D1446326

fie

TRAVELS TO THE ENU

Jakov Lind

TRAVELS
TO THE ENU

STORY OF A SHIPWRECK

St. Martin's Press/ Marek
New York

Copyright © 1982 by Jakov Lind
For information, write: St. Martin's Press
175 Fifth Avenue, New York, N.Y. 10010
Manufactured in the United States of America

Library of Congress Cataloging in Publication Data

Lind, Jakov, 1927-
Travels to the Enu.

I. Title.

| PR6062.I45T68 | 1982 | 823′.914 | 81-21457 |
| ISBN 0-312-81630-8 | | AACR2 | |

First published in Great Britain by Eyre Methuen Ltd.

For Annie Truxell, who paints it all

Acknowledgements

To all seafaring travellers into unknown worlds, above all to our Master, Jonathan Swift, acknowledgement is due.

To Geoffrey Strachan, editor and publisher and friend, who has helped me with patience, my sincere and heartfelt thanks.

For there are some persons who believe there are many worlds, and some who even fancy that they are boundless in extent, being themselves inexperienced and ignorant of the truth of those things of which it is desirable to have a correct knowledge.

Philo Judaeus (c. 25 B.C.–c. A.D. 45)

. . . and in the midst there is the tree of life in that place, on which God rests when he comes into paradise. And this tree cannot be described for its excellence and sweet odour.

Enoch (A.D. 1–50)

One

When I reached Crownflights in Baker Street that Tuesday afternoon, walking through pouring rain without an umbrella, I was surprised to find it open. It was about 2 p.m. and, whether or not this was due to the weather, there was no one else in the shop. Usually Crownflights is crowded with lonely, silent figures waiting their turn to ask at length how to get to Dubrovnik by a combination of bus and train. Crownflights serves our immediate neighbourhood which is peopled by poor clerks, small shopkeepers and many lonely widows of modest means and offers the cheapest charter flights anywhere in town.

The clerk who served me, John Farquharson, a well-groomed young Scot with blond hair down to his shoulders, drew my attention to a poster he had just put up right opposite the entrance, above and behind his counter. 'COSMIC TAKES GOOD CARE OF YOU. Southampton–Sarawak–Southampton £650 – no extras. Departure soon. Book now.'

'Seems a bit cheap, Mr Farquharson, don't you think?'

'It's a bargain, Mr Orlando, I don't know how they do it.'

He handed me a brochure. It showed the waving palms of Sarawak, native huts on stilts, dark smiling faces, and a blue and white painted pleasure vessel called the S.S. *Katherine Medici*, close up.

'Six hundred and fifty pounds for four months? Ridiculous price, Mr Farquharson.'

'Tax not included, sir. All in all it will be more like six

hundred and ninety-five pounds, and seven pence, if I'm not mistaken.'

'Still too cheap. Tell me honestly. Where is the trap?'

'No trap. No trick. No hitch. Not as far as I can tell, sir. All above board, all straightforward. It's a new thing called "social tourism". Sleep on it. Don't decide now but think about it, and let me know by tomorrow afternoon at the latest, please. We seem to be getting a lot of bookings. The price is good. Lord knows where people learned of it so fast. Must have been in the papers. I didn't notice. Social tourism! What next! Think about it. They might not be your kind of people, Mr Orlando. You might find no one to your taste, no one to talk to.'

I went straight home to think about it. Four months in the safe belly of a pleasure boat surrounded by nice ordinary people with no one to talk to! No more brains, no more geniuses, no more prophets! To dissolve into an ocean of unpretentious humanity – what a blissful idea! What a unique opportunity to open a mine of untapped personal stories. Three meals a day, a bed, a table, a lamp. My own cabin and nowhere to go to but either up on deck to listen and eat or down below to write and sleep. *Paradise* or *Travels Beyond the Horizon* was to be the working title of my book. On Wednesday I was just about to go to Crownflights shortly before lunchtime, to pay a deposit or purchase a ticket, whatever seemed necessary to assure me a place on this heavenly barge, when Trevor was on the phone.

'I want to say goodbye.'

'Where are you going?'

'I am leaving on a boat called the *Katherine Medici*, I like the name, sailing for Sarawak. She is supposed to put in on Pikauri in the Paasch Islands, where I get off. I have a job with the British–Fiji Friendship Society, doing research on an abandoned island which was used for nuclear testing. Tell you more about it when I am back. So long for now.'

'Trevor, it seems we are on the same boat. I too am leaving for Sarawak with the same *Katherine Medici* next week.'

'Strange coincidence – but, believe me, things will get much stranger. I have been in that part of the world before. You'll see.'

'I'll see you on board, Trevor.'

'Don't let it worry you if you don't.'

Used to sloppy waiters and rude cabin attendants who hate their employers, their jobs, and of course those they have to serve, I at first noticed nothing uncommon on board. The sight of the crew lolling on the sundeck all day long, teamugs of beer in their right hands, cigarettes in their left, chatting the hours away while we had to make our own beds, clean our cabins and toilets, serve ourselves at table and, if we wanted a clean plate, go and wash it ourselves, had many passengers confused as to whether or not service was included in the all-in fare. Very gradually I came to feel that there was indeed something exceedingly strange about this ship, though what it was I couldn't exactly say.

Trevor, whom I had expected to meet, had obviously not made it; something must have happened at the last moment. Had he shown up I would have seen him. It is impossible to avoid a face after forty-eight hours on the same ship. No Trevor, no one to talk to, except the gloomiest of all prophets of gloom, a small man, with the mousy eyes of a wizard, my chess partner Peter Lockwood, a retired railway engineer from Bristol. Every night after dinner we went to our table in the Beau Brummel saloon and played our eight or ten games of 'Blitz', a game that allows no time for meditating a move.

'Harry Bolding was in my class at Pitweth Primary.'

'Who is Harry Bolding?'

'Bolding is Mr Cosmic Limited, that's who he is. He owns our bloody lives, not just this floating coffin.'

'What floating coffin?'

'Crafty bugger he was even back at school. We called him " 'Arry the 'orse". Ahead of every one of us and, as you can see, still is. Trapped us with his bloody social tourism – goes down well with idiots like ourselves.'

13

'Social tourism, what's that?'

'Haven't read the brochure, eh?'

'Of course I did, I have it right here in my pocket.'

Of course I hadn't read it but planned to do so the next time I was queuing up for my morning tea.

'Read the small print on page eighteen?'

I leafed to page eighteen and there it said: 'Cosmic Ltd. are pioneers in social tourism. We herald the tourism of the future. An experience of a lifetime, a unique experiment in human relationships. Only Cosmic offers its passengers a working holiday and its crew a well-earned rest simultaneously. Social tourism teaches us how to live like men of the sea, and to acquire the wisdom and tranquillity of the seafarer. For detailed scale of remuneration of working passengers please turn over but meanwhile welcome to our beautiful lady *Katherine Medici* on her maiden voyage.'

When I looked up, Lockwood quickly glanced away, pretending he had not watched me as I studied the Cosmic message.

'Us do the work for the crew, what next?'

'We are all doing it and so are you. Don't you clean up your own mess in your cabin?'

'I thought they were on strike.'

'That's no strike, Mr Orlando, that's the system. The system hits at our love of comfort. Social tourism is the game.'

'It's a disaster,' I heard myself say, solemnly.

Lockwood had been pretending not to listen.

'What disaster are you referring to? Anyway, why worry now that it's too late in any case?'

'You mean to say we can't get off?'

'There is no getting off, only down, sir. There are no ports of call.'

'Here it says on page fifteen: Mombasa, Djibouti, Lagos, Madagascar, Bombay, Capetown, Calcutta, and Djakarta.'

'And all for six hundred and fifty quid? Bolding's not a charity. He couldn't do it, not even for double the fare.'

'So what's going to become of us?'

14

'I am no prophet. You can figure it out for yourself.'

I pondered whether disaster had to be my inevitable fate so early on my road to paradise. Maybe I could, or rather we could, all of us, change our situation at the last moment, just as a brilliant move may save a seemingly lost game. Alas, I couldn't think of anything.

According to Lockwood our situation was absolutely hopeless. Bolding had no charter to sail the ship, his charter had been withdrawn pending the outcome of litigation against him. The ship had been sealed by the port authority. Bolding had only one option: bribe the guards, sail her out, scuttle her somewhere away from commonly used sea lanes and claim insurance.

Margaret Thatcher was not about to send the Royal Navy after us. Bet? Hadn't I observed how fast they had processed nine hundred and thirty-four passengers through customs and immigration? All palms were greased, that was fairly obvious. I hadn't noticed anything. Like everyone else I didn't want to miss the boat and was glad we could board so quickly.

'To be quite honest, Mr Orlando, I, too, made a mistake. I knew all this beforehand but I always find it hard to believe in my own sombre forecasts. I had my first real shock when I discovered who our captain is. Gilbert Cook.'

'Who is Gilbert Cook?'

'Who is Gilbert Cook? Where have you been, sir? Don't you read the papers? Gilbert Cook is on parole from Dartmoor prison where he had another twenty years to serve for manslaughter.'

'What did he do?'

'He claims it was negligence – but the prosecuting Counsel could prove he had sealed doors and windows, turned on the gas, and left the house, while the family was sound asleep. Grandparents, wife and four children.'

'He gassed them? What a gruesome tale, Mr Lockwood! Your Bristol sense of humour, I take it.'

'Bristol sense of humour, my foot. Cook is a murderer.

Ichabod, the purser, is a known underworld figure from Soho. John Hodensack, Cook's first officer, is a sadistic homosexual killer. Papa Brown, the Jamaican first cook with the harelip, did his mother in and so I could go on, Mr Orlando.'

'Thanks, Mr Lockwood, that will do fine for today.'

Nothing happened until Friday that might be called odd or exciting. On Saturday morning at breakfast the Wetherall sisters from Torquay, Mary and Betty (one had blue the other pink dyed hair) told the table of a missing gold ring and diamond necklace after Petty Officer Sean Boramwood paid them a short visit.

Ichabod, the purser, had promised an investigation, but the sisters were in tears all the same. This 'rude fellow' had actually dared to suggest that they were after the insurance money.

Our table tried in vain to console the sobbing sisters, suggesting that they might after all have mislaid their jewellery. Lockwood was firm on the subject. 'First your money, then your clothes. So it goes. What do you expect from pirates? Soon it'll get worse. Just you wait.'

We were half way down the African coast. The coast we saw briefly, in a haze. Our speed was 35 knots. The stories of pilfering and petty theft by the crew began to multiply like the cockroaches and rats in the filthy kitchens and dining-rooms. Most passengers stopped working and the crew didn't care a damn whether we did or not. How much longer could this go on and where was it all going to end? Lectured and preached at by Peter Lockwood our table had turned into a philosophical seminary. 'Things that go badly tend to get worse. They must get rid of us now because we know too much. Resign yourself to your fate and feel like the bloody coward you are or stand up for yourself and have your head blown off. There is nothing we can do to change our situation.'

Lockwood made us miserable, frustrated and depressed. Only a few days (and it seemed like a lifetime) ago, meal-

16

times had been a time for endless anecdotes and jokes. No longer.

When Thomas Cullen was first reported to have disappeared, I thought Lockwood, who told the story with a certain glee in his voice, had gone too far.

'Thomas Cullen was a retired schoolteacher from Reading. This same Cullen had been headmaster at Dartington Hall and was sacked for writing passionate love letters to a twelve-year-old boy, who boastfully showed them to his classmates. Barely twenty yards away from the restaurant on 'B' Deck Cullen was robbed of his wallet by two masked men. When he reported it to Ichabod he was told the wallet had been found and apparently nothing was missing from it. To thank and maybe reward the honest finder the old bugger suggested Cullen should come for drinks to his cabin. During the course of two hours, "drinks" turned into a drunken homosexual orgy, complete with leather masks, chains, spikes, and whips. By 3 a.m. poor Cullen, who has a heart condition, passes away. Two naked sailors were seen dumping his naked body overboard.'

After Cullen hadn't shown up at our table for three days, we began to believe Lockwood. Paul de Groot, the Dutchman from Swansea, and his girlfriend Ellen went to Ichabod to ask what might have happened to Cullen. The morning after they showed us their black and blue bruises. They were kicked and beaten by drunken crew members, shortly after midnight. They had forgotten to lock their door. Things got rapidly worse. Within a few days to be beaten up for asking questions was a mere bagatelle, compared to the violence the crew used against those who clung to their wallets and jewels. People hardly dared to walk the decks but would march in columns of twelve to protect themselves against lurking crew members. There were plenty of fist fights. One had to be on one's guard at all times – against the passengers, as well as the crew.

Lockwood stated the obvious as usual, just to give us an additional taste of horror. 'The bastards have finally declared war on us now. It's all out in the open. Watch out. They'll try to hit us in the guts first. Where it hurts most. An empty stomach turns a man into a wild dog, he loses his self-respect – then his enemy can kill him and feel morally superior for having done so.'

Within a couple of days Lockwood's prophecies came true. The beef-steaks were down to two ounces. Potatoes, rice and vegetables were only distributed to those over sixty-five and under fourteen. The first ugly scenes started over sugar and cornflakes at breakfast, with a grabbing and pushing such as none of us could remember, not even at the height of rationing at the end of World War II. In those days, people would still say: 'I am so sorry' after treading on your toes. Now the most commonly used phrase was 'Take your foot off mine or you'll be sorry.'

'Artificially created shortages divide the rich from the poor, the strong from the weak, the corrupt from the honest and the shrewd bastards among us from our more simple-minded brethren,' was Lockwood's oracular observation. 'If every man fights for himself, you can control the lot' – along with other such lapidary wisecracks. But what could be done, in fact and not just in theory, about the disappearance of milk, coffee and tea, which were replaced by Ovaltine and herbal teas (better for our health, it was suggested), short of using a physical force we did not possess, not even the all-knowing Lockwood could tell.

Instead of an answer he offered us more and more of his depressing forecasts. 'We shall soon all be down with the fishes. We asked for it, didn't we? No one forced us, we came of our own accord, didn't we? In any case, whether we came of our own free will or not – all that's left now is to ponder whether there will be a resurrection for ordinary sinners and what this resurrection might be like.'

Salt, ketchup, pepper, mustard vanished and soon afterwards the beer at the bar went up from forty pence to a pound a pint. A shot of Cutty Sark was suddenly two pounds, a rum and Coke was three pounds fifty. Alcohol was soon out of reach of most pockets, which was probably just as well, on our empty stomachs, and was also good for our livers. Drinking water was available but for twenty pence (or fifty cents) a glass, and you needed a friend behind the counter to get it by the pint or gallon. At a pound a pint or eight pounds a gallon most people swallowed their saliva or made do with their ration of two cups of herbal tea a day.

What we believed was the Cape of Good Hope vanished in blue mist and now we were speeding for the wide Indian Ocean, at 45 knots. It was obvious we had been hijacked in one of the most daring and original feats of piracy, and no one at our table, not even Lockwood, knew of another case in maritime criminal history in which nine hundred-odd paying passengers on a pleasure cruise had been shanghaied by their captain and crew. Our chances of saving our lives and possessions had dwindled to nil.

'The days of redeeming your life with money are gone for good,' Lockwood preached. 'You can no longer pay with money for your life, that's clear. If someone wants your life, you don't have to sell it; he pays you for it, what it's worth. A fig.' To illustrate the value of a fig he stuck his thumb between index and middle finger.

Though all and everything seemed lost, there were still a great number of serious-looking respectable people among us who believed it wasn't too late to talk to Cook about our grievances. We elected a Passengers' Action Committee. The name alone dispensed two days of hope to the faint-hearted. 'The Committee' (for short) made an appointment to see the Captain on a Friday evening at 8 p.m. sharp.

Gilbert Cook was a man best avoided. He had fair, thin hair hanging straight from an elongated skull, the shifty looks of a cornered rat, thin lips, a weak chin and the pointed nose of a vindictive gremlin. Delighted by his unappealing exterior, Cook cherished it the way a chameleon does its mimicry. As the cynics had foreseen and the optimists had refused to believe, Cook was unmoved by our pleas. He let everyone have his say, listened patiently, while looking us straight in the eye and never showed any emotion. When it was finally his turn to speak he flashed his large yellow horse teeth and said with controlled anger that Cosmic Ltd. had forced him to sail without sufficient funds, without pre-arranged credits, for reasons that were none of our business and of which he himself was ignorant. Instead of looking for scapegoats we would do better to be realistic. Stocks had dwindled, provisions had to be rationed, fuel and water had reached emergency reserves. The ship's finances were a total disaster and if the passengers did not come forward voluntarily soon and put up the funds, force would have to be applied to extract what was needed in order to avoid a calamity.

'It's time for concrete sacrifices, ladies and gentlemen. We have talked enough.' With these cool words, Cook dismissed the Committee, wishing every one of us the best of British luck. When the Committee returned with the bad news despair changed into resignation and mourning, self-reproach and self-pity. From now on all the optimists looked naive and silly and Lockwood's words were quoted like the sayings of a sage: 'No one will ever believe our story and none of us will be there to tell it.' Yet for two days nothing more was heard about the 'concrete sacrifices'. Then came the afternoon of trial, as Lockwood called it afterwards.

The sirens summoned us to the top deck. We were lined up in long rows. A voice boomed: 'Shut up!' Everyone fell silent and Cook's voice came over the loudspeaker from afar, like the voice of a celestial judge.

'Sacrifices will have to be made at short notice. The fate of the individual is linked to the well-being of our entire community. Social responsibility means abandoning the idea of private possessions, together with everything else. To save our souls, ladies and gentlemen, I suggest you give everything up. Hand it over. Sacrifice! Sacrifice!'

After this little speech, sailors holding up black plastic dustbin liners walked from one person to the next. We were asked to hold our hands above our heads and were frisked.

The bags soon filled up, with purses and wallets, watches and jewellery. No one had the courage to refuse, except David Atherton, a truly lone hero.

Among a mass of cowards there is always one man or woman who refuses to be coerced and hates to do anything that is not of his own free will. David Atherton, sixty-five, retired bank manager at Lloyds' Putney Bridge Branch, had earned a number of service medals for bravery in the face of the enemy in the past, among them the Victoria Cross for valour at Dunkirk in June 1940, when he helped evacuate our boys who were trapped on the beaches of Normandy, exposed to the merciless attacks of Stukas, which swooped down on them like hungry hawks on a yard filled with mice. Atherton at that time sailed his small pleasure craft back and forth across the Channel, was wounded, capsized and nearly drowned several times, and practically bled to death when a shell splinter pierced his lung. He had a history. With the fearless glare of the righteous, he bellowed out so loud that even the seagulls fell silent: 'No sir. Over my dead body.'

There was a minute's silence. Cook was stunned by this single man's revolt. He blinked once or twice. Prometheus had risen against his father Zeus but alas this time the outcome was going to be different. It was too late for revolt. Cook and his officers knew it and so did Atherton. I could see it on his face; he was standing only a few feet away from me. Now it slowly dawned on him that the time for heroes had passed. He began to twitch, he started to laugh nervously. I can still see him looking like a burning torch in his red jogging suit, legs apart, as solid as his own monument in stone.

He pointed an accusing finger at Cook, who did not tolerate this long. He jerked his head to the right, as if he were shaking a fly off his neck. From God knows where, four strong sailors emerged, grabbing Atherton with iron fists and turned him upside down. They shook him as one shakes a sack for the last potato to tumble out. They frisked him and found only the key to his cabin. Then they carried him, still upside down, lifted him high over the railing and simply heaved him overboard. His voice rose faintly once more: 'Help me you idiots! Do something!' but then it faded into a gurgle and was drowned in the noise of the propeller. Most of us looked down at our feet. A few ardent Catholics went on their knees and crossed themselves. And that was the end of Atherton, the last of the heroes.

After Atherton's death, the ship was turned into an armed camp. Wherever we went, at each entrance and exit, silent armed sailors with their hands in their pockets, watched every single step we made. Most people remained in their cabins to wait and pray.

Three days passed and nothing happened. Then one Wednesday morning four people were found dangling from a cable that ran from the starboard mast to the funnel. On the notice board in the main lobby a note appeared: *'Warning: Take note! Craig Milton, 70; his wife Grace, 65; Philip St John, 60; Peter Prem, 84, were caught redhanded looting the storage rooms. They were tried, found guilty, and hanged as a warning to all passengers. Signed: Cook.'*

As we moved south of the tropic of Capricorn, the whole ship soon began to smell. The four were unceremoniously cut down and buried at sea while prayers were said over the Public Announcement System. Two days later, Cook must have decided his crew's morale might suffer from further public executions. It was time to tone things down. His madness had reached its zenith. Or so we thought. Duped by our own despair, we believed we could observe signs of rebellion among the sailors and some more forthcoming officers. There was gossip about a mutiny. Some of us claimed to have heard and seen unusual activities.

Then suddenly came a rapid move towards normality. We received four slices of bread at breakfast instead of two. Milk, sugar and cereals turned up. Most of us remained sceptical, but when honey and strawberry jam reappeared, there were repeated rounds of applause. Lockwood, of course, wasn't impressed by anything that smacked of improvement. 'If things ever seem to be getting better, watch out. Things that go badly tend to get worse, that much we know by now. Even if some things seem to be improving, everything must ultimately end in catastrophe.'

Lockwood was hated by now and had to stay in his cabin. Yet fact is fact. Milk was back in the Ovaltine and sugar back on the cornflakes. People were talking of soft- and hard-boiled eggs, peanut butter and bacon and the imminent return of potatoes; their mood contradicted Lockwood's pessimism. The words 'ice cream' and 'pudding' were heard again. To top everything the weather was beautiful. Bets were made on the date the old cuppa would flow once more. The armed sentries had disappeared, one by one. Someone believed he had seen land. Others said either a mutiny or something of the kind was brewing. We felt strangely unobserved. The crew had vanished below decks.

'Watch out. They're doing it to fool us,' Lockwood whispered.

'How do you explain the fact that Cook and his pals haven't had their throats cut by the crew by now, Mr Lockwood, the way Cook treats them?'

'They're not a crew, these dogs! At the slightest sign of a mutiny he'll massacre the lot of them. Let's face it, sir. The crew are dogs and we are cattle. Haven't you noticed how cosy we're all getting together? Just like cattle in the cowshed. We rub each others' backs and wait for what happens next. Will they milk us, feed us, let us out, cut our throats? Without guns to defend ourselves we are animals before the slaughter, not human beings. Fortunately our troubles will soon be over, and nothing matters any more; the great butcher awaits us all!'

Four days passed. Lockwood was out of favour with everyone again. There was not plenty but there was now adequate food and polite if not friendly relations between crew and passengers. And if this weren't enough, four among the fourteen at our table, myself among them, were one day handed small gilt-edged cards requesting the pleasure of our company at the Captain's table. From what I could gather Cook had invited two kinds of guests. One he called 'flunkies' or 'arselickers', the other kind 'prophets of doom'. To receive an invitation you had to belong to one of these two categories. Lockwood, who was not invited, wished us luck and went off to sleep. At 8 p.m. sharp, twenty-four of us filed in. The table was laid for a banquet. Silver, flowers and champagne in ice buckets. Silent, white-gloved, uniformed waiters. One could imagine the Prime Minister or a visiting member of the Royal Family was about to appear. This was obviously not the regular setting for dinner but a gala occasion. Cook proposed a short toast to her Majesty the Queen, Prince Philip, Prince Charles and his bride, Princess Anne and the rest of the Royal Family – something which always goes down well in times of crisis. Monarchist sentiments always cleanse and soothe.

When it came to the coffee, the sweets and the cognac, the conversation, or rather Cook's monologue, touched upon two subjects. The first was that stocks, shares, promissory notes, property deeds and wills might be legally made over to his name, providing all necessary papers were signed in his presence. The other topic was the mysterious disappearance of single ships and entire convoys within certain magnetic triangles that appeared to exist everywhere, and not just in the Caribbean. 'Ships do disappear. They vanish from one moment to the next and are never seen or heard of again; that's the truth.'

At about 1 a.m. I left the table, my head spinning thanks to an excessive consumption of alcohol and food. I was totally drunk and felt sick. I wanted to discuss the evening with Lockwood but his lights were out. I decided it could wait. As soon as I laid my head on my bunk I was out too.

At about 5 a.m. I heard seven short and three long blasts of the ship's siren. The frantic signals of the fire alarm. My cabin door was flung open. Eddie Nose, Alfie Bean and Len Talbot stood in the door. Eddie Nose is six foot three and has a squashed nose he blames on an unfortunate encounter with an Irishman in a Piraeus bar many years ago. Alfie Bean was one of the two men who had thrown Cullen overboard. He has the reputation of having killed a German tourist in London over the old argument of whether Allied air raids could be compared to German atrocities. A good question. He was sentenced for manslaughter, later escaped, went to Australia where he met his pal, curly-headed Len Talbot, Australian world champion beer drinker who downs twenty-two pints in eleven minutes, forty-five seconds and is mentioned in *The Guinness Book of Records*. Only a day or so previously Talbot had offered me a bottle of Scotch in exchange for my boots, but suggested he was in no hurry for the deal as he would get the boots sooner or later anyway. It looked as if the time had come to hand them over.

The three wore battle fatigues with several buttons missing. They didn't say a word, just looked at me. I got out of bed and dressed. Over the intercom came the final instalment of unadulterated madness. 'Ladies and gentlemen. This is a special announcement. During the early hours of this morning we have been invaded and occupied by seaborne guerrillas of the PLA, the Polynesian Liberation Army. The Polynesian Liberation Forces are struggling to liberate their homeland, Tasmania, from the colonialist, imperialist fetters of a bygone age. All of us on board, men, women and children; officers, passengers and crew; in short, every single one of us is being held hostage by the forces of Polynesian Liberation until the plenary session of the General Assembly of the United Nations, which is about to meet in New York within a few hours, decides whether or not to debate the future of the enslaved people of Tasmania. Our fate, ladies and gentlemen, is no longer in our hands, but is being decided for us on the other side of the globe. Meanwhile soldiers of the PLA will collect all your personal belongings, trunks, suitcases, bags and parcels and search them for valuables to help finance their war of liberation. Holders of stocks and shares, wills, promissory notes and other papers will be given the chance to sign them over to me, your lawful authority.

Exempt from confiscation are walking aids for the infirm and elderly and personal wigs and dentures. To facilitate the search all cabins are to be evacuated immediately. All passengers must assemble on 'A' Deck within five minutes of now. It is in your very best interests to comply with this order. This is an announcement on behalf of Polynesian Liberation.'

'A' Deck looked like a first aid station immediately after a severe earthquake: hundreds of shivering figures in their nightclothes with their arms wrapped round them, trembling, mostly barefoot, unwashed, uncombed, with their hair in curlers and without make-up. Despite permission, many had left their dentures and others their glasses behind. What a spectacle! Cries, sighs, gasps. Papa Brown stepped on to a chair dressed in battle fatigues, surrounded by familiar faces. For this Polynesian charade, Cook had chosen as many blacks and coloureds as he could find on board. They pointed the barrels of their machine guns at us, which according to Lockwood were not loaded, though I wouldn't have taken a bet on it. Larry Lewis, from Trinidad, referred to Papa Brown as 'Marshall Papaver' and to himself as 'Colonel Mango'. He pretended to translate the garbled nonsense that came from 'Papaver's' lips. It was pidgin French, supposed to be Polynesian. 'Marshall Papaver' screamed, hissed and yelled or whispered incomprehensible syllables, gesticulated with both arms, and shook his body and head till his eyes nearly popped out of their sockets. 'Colonel Mango' translated: 'Men and women, friends and comrades. We have been exploited by the imperialist–zionist forces of Satan. We are fighting to free ourselves from a yoke of perpetual evil. We suffer humiliation, hunger and deprivation, like no other nation on earth. Now we are standing up for ourselves and presenting you with a choice. Co-operate with us or be damned. Co-operate or we'll send you back to hell where you all came from. Co-operate or you will be badly hurt. This is "Operation Clean-Up", and we have come to clean up.'

26

This went on for more than ten minutes. A charade of common prejudice plus pure nonsense and a near-verbatim rendering of all the commonest clichés in the papers. Suddenly it was all over. Tapes played a tango over the loudspeakers. We were allowed to return to our cabins. 'Operation Clean-up' had resulted in our cabins being now totally empty except for the rubbish they had left behind. Even our reading matter, the old copies of *Time* and *Newsweek*, *Vogue* and *Playboy*, was gone. We stared at the walls; nothing to read. My mind had gone blank. Too stunned to think or move, everyone in his own cubicle was probably now praying for a swift delivery from this ultimate nightmare.

Shortly after 6 p.m. when we had been locked up for over four hours without food or blankets, Cook's voice returned through the ceiling and was heralded by the opening bars of Beethoven's Fifth. 'Ladies and gentlemen. Once more, this is your Captain speaking. For no apparent reason, the terrorist raiders suddenly abandoned ship and sped away in their junks. Loyal officers gave chase, killed most of them, and have recovered their entire booty. But now comes even better news. Previous calculations of the ship's reserves were wilfully underestimated. Those responsible for this act of sabotage will sooner or later be brought to justice. Meanwhile I am happy to announce the immediate release of the following items: lamb, pork and beef; carrot juice and grapefruit segments; fried and roast chicken; cold turkey, smoked and cooked salmon; vanilla ice cream; chocolate pudding; apple pie; marshmallow; frozen strawberries; orange sherbet; cheesecake.'

I couldn't listen to all this and turned it off. I went to see Lockwood. He seemed mesmerized. He was pointing a finger up at the ceiling from which Cook's voice boomed out. It was the first time I had seen him with a radiant look over his entire face. He seemed a changed person. His eyes sparkled. 'Listen to that, Mr Orlando.'

'. . . The rationing of drinking water is to be abolished until further notice. We have plenty of water on board. We are approaching Sarawak. Anyone who wishes to disembark here can do so. We will direct him or her to the British Consul, who will only be too pleased to arrange your return passage to Britain. Anyone momentarily short of cash should not be timid but rest assured our Consul has the necessary funds reserved for such emergencies.'

In the background a choir sang 'For He's a Jolly Good Fellow!' to the strains of a piano.

'How about that, Mr Orlando? How about that?' Lockwood was transfixed. His face had taken on an angelic expression.

'It's going to be a lot of fun . . . Oh boy . . .' Lockwood's speech was once more interrupted by Cook's voice:

'And now, ladies and gentlemen, it's time to celebrate. Let me invite you all to a big party around the swimming pool tonight. Prepare for your second baptism. We are crossing the line. We are skipping Saturday. It's Friday now. In a few hours it will be Sunday. Make of it what you will. We have trying times behind us. Let us not dwell on them. Our ordeal has proved the virtue of persistence. The worst is over. We'll all have a few drinks and a good laugh. We have made it to Sarawak, half way around the world.'

'You hear that? He is sending us to hell. He and his cronies will probably take off. There must be an island nearby. God knows where we are. We have no radio communication. We have neither a transmitter nor a receiver on board. Never had them. We are nowhere.'

A few minutes later Elvis Presley was on the intercom, to warm us up for tonight's party.

Then suddenly the rock music faded, and Cook's voice was back for the last time now.

'A last word of farewell from your skipper, ladies and gentlemen. To prepare a rip-roaring reception for you in Sarawak some of my officers and some of the crew will accompany me in a motor launch. We shall depart ahead of you in maybe half an hour, but before darkness falls. Let me give you a bit of serious advice with regard to the use of fireworks tonight.

In current circumstances it is not advisable for you to light as much as a match. The terrorists have left plastic explosives in corners where they are hard to detect. Be careful! And now, to all of you I say farewell and the very best of British luck. End of message.'

'No, I couldn't have invented it.' I agreed with Lockwood. I couldn't have made this one up.

'What now? Like to have a game of chess?'

The Polynesians had overlooked one chessboard, or not knowing what to do with it had simply left it behind. It was Lockwood's turn to play white. He moved his queen's pawn to queen four, I moved my knight to the classic Koslov defence. Lockwood raced his queen's bishop. I put my other knight forward. Lockwood made an opening for his queen's bishop to pass, which was definitely the wrong move. Was he playing to lose? Did he want me to win? I suddenly lost interest in the game but couldn't tell why.

'I am going up on deck, I want to see the buggers leave.'

'I like it where I am,' was the last I heard of Peter Lockwood.

Two

And that's how on Sunday morning, shortly before 4 a.m., on 15th February 1980, the SS *Katherine Medici* entered her final port of call, a permanent darkness eight thousand feet below the surface, and took her 934 paying passengers, her crew of 180 men, her 36 officers and her captain, who didn't get away in time after all, down with her. She must have been rotten through and through, a sapless mummy, dry as a bone. It took her no more than twelve minutes to vanish under the dark mirror. After her lights went out one by one, a translucent full moon the size of a giant yellow filter went down after her. An eerie white light remained for a few minutes but quickly dissolved into an early morning mist, the stars receded upwards into the spheres, a light drizzle came down, sounds of splashing, gurgling water moving back and forth.

As the shore came closer, the outgoing tide dragged me back by my feet. Icy-cold undercurrents rushed over me and under me until the surf got hold of me, lifted me up, held me on its crest for a few short moments and finally hurled me ashore. A painful delivery, but at last I felt the ground under my feet. Ahead of me was a pink light and, as if all the world had been held up close to a celestial sunlamp for quick results, black greys and purples turned into various shades of green. To my left, a few hundred yards up the coast, I believed I could see one, then two, and then two more figures wading through the low tide. I was not sure if they saw me, but I was certain they went down on their knees, one after the other, and finally fell forward in slow motion and vanished out of sight. A few seconds later I, too, must have passed out.

I woke from the chill of early morning surrounded by a forest of dark, thin legs. I scrambled to my feet, still dazed from exhaustion, cold and shock, and to my amazement I found myself facing a crowd of the most unbelievable creatures. At first I thought I must have landed amidst a tribe of hominid baboons. Noses and mouths formed a single snout. Their big, brown cow-like eyes gave them that particular look of slave and savage I had seen so often before in my life, but could not for the moment locate. Foreheads, cheeks, and necks were painted in flaming reds, greens, purples and oranges. Their necks, arms, wrists and ankles were heavily weighted down with charms and amulets of all shapes and sizes, made from the usual shells, stones and feathers of birds of paradise. In addition to these, some had leathery objects dangling from their middles; a shrunken head, an arm, or a foot. These trophies and amulets gave them a human touch that their faces belied. What seemed even odder was that these dark brown and honey-coloured natives had reddish pink penises, fairly long and thin, attached to heavy brown testicles the size of tennis balls. Their behinds, too, were probably meant to simulate the backsides of baboons. They were painted in light red and iridescent peacock green, with formidable bulges, definitely human and not simian, to judge by their shape.

The men had their hair stacked high in fuzzy, towering constructions, which at first glance looked like birds' nests and which, to my surprise, on closer examination, turned out to be used for that very purpose. Most of the men in the front rows carried birds that were quite large; strange birds, some of them similar to pigeons in size, while others had eagles and vultures, herons, storks and cranes, buzzards and pelicans nestling on top of them. It soon became apparent that only the males wore these birds' nests. The females braided their long sleek, black hair, which was not at all fuzzy like their men's hair, into a single plait, which was probably used as a means of catching hold of them.

It was easy to distinguish what looked like two different species of females, two totally different physical types. One kind stood firmly tall and handsome, on shapely legs, and had well-formed breasts, bellies, and arms, while the second type swayed uncertainly on small bowlegs, had spotted and wrinkled skin, eyebrows which met together, and a sickly yellow colour to the whites of their eyes. Their bellies were bloated, their breasts deflated, their necks seemed made of sponge. They wore the ends of ropes around their ankles and were probably the slaves of their haughty-looking sisters. I saw a few small children – most of them had shaven scalps except for a lengthy tuft of hair – and a few young male teenagers with parrots or owls on their heads. It was a colourful first encounter with what seemed to me a very rare and very forlorn tribe.

As I smiled at them, they all smiled back at me, as if by command. Their thin lips revealed regular rows of gleaming white teeth filed down to sharp points. A shoal of hungry barracudas on human legs would scare anyone, I consoled myself, not just me. So far nothing had frightened me in these new surroundings except this eerie smile. However strange it may seem, the moment I had hit the water I had felt instantly more invigorated, even ebullient, and more foolishly fearless than I had ever felt in my life before.

In the process of fighting my fear of sharks, being an inexperienced swimmer, I had also rid myself of a lethargy which must have been pressing down on me with a heavy hand for many more years than I care to remember. Now after having the sensation of no ground under my feet, all of a sudden I felt level-headed, determined, good humoured, relaxed, and even cheerful. Far from feeling lost, I felt safe, as safe as I was, in fact.

I had not realized what suddenly being shipwrecked can do to the nervous system. I was to do so much later, but not at the time. I didn't know that this type of shock can make you hallucinate, see mirages, make you hear a plane over-head searching the seas for survivors. I also believed for some reason that I was far from lost in limbo but had an exact, or more or less exact idea of my location at a latitude of 60 degrees 53 minutes. Therefore I should have been some-where between Magasay and Captain Farlow's Island, 2500 nautical miles to the south-east of the Solomons, a remote spot on the atlas, far from Southampton; remote but not removed from the dimension I live in.

And while the tribe that surrounded me on this strange Sunday morning was hardly known in anthropological circles, its existence is certainly documented in the log of Dr Tomaso Silva de Goncales, King Esteban II of Portugal's private troubleshooter to Timor, who was sent out to uncover an anti-Royalist plot and ended up living for over a year among them – the very same Enu who now confronted me. This was back in 1742 – and since then not a single explorer had ever found the way down to Enu Island again. It had been mysteriously erased from existence. The only map of it there had ever been was probably on board the SS *Katherine Medici*. Enough said.

'The Enu of the Kawflick Atoll,' wrote the Doctor, 'are not only infamous for cutting off their enemies' limbs to decorate themselves, but are probably the only ungodly or pagan tribe in the world to be ruled by an aviary of multi-coloured birds.'

It was this that explained the flapping and fluttering of so many wings before my eyes and the excessive noise which arose from a crowd of people who hardly opened their mouths. For, as it says on page one of the *Observaciones de una Alma Perdate* (the doctor became a mystic after his return to Portugal), 'Just as we in Europe and in the Americas are owned and possessed by our cattle and horses; our sheep, goats and pigs; our cats and dogs; chickens and geese; and all the rest of the livestock of civilized husbandry, so the Enu of the

Kawflick Atoll are overlorded by birds of many types of plumage and beak, which at some unknown point in their history, gained ascendancy over the entire male population. We in Europe, in our shameful naiveté, believe our so-called domestic animals to be our property, while it would be more truthful to say that it is these shrewd quadrupeds who domesticate, exploit, and possess us in their unmitigated selfishness; for they are, as we know, with their corporeal nature, the brute creations of the Animal Kingdom . . .'

And so he goes on, lecturing us about our relationship with animals, until by page five you begin to realize that what the doctor had in mind was a political pamphlet, a fable disguised as an adventure story – and that he probably never left his verandah overlooking the Timor Sea.

At the end of his thirty-page booklet he claims that after he had lived for a year among the Enu they sold him to British pirates for a pound of tobacco and two pipes. On page twenty-three de Goncales, who must have been a pedantic eighteenth-century scientist, describes a ritual that I never had the chance to witness. In his own words: 'Every male firstborn of good and noble family is eligible for CHUFFA one of the most unusual rites among the pagans I have so far visited on my travels. The young boy, aged six or seven, accompanied by his father and brother or another close relative, submits himself to a strange form of initiation. While his young companions hold his mouth open, an URUPA, a holy bird, pecks and mutilates his tongue. Not more than one small peck at a time – the ritual is a monthly occurrence and ends when the child (by this time a young man of about fourteen) speaks with the same impediments as his mentors, a language entirely incomprehensible to the rest of the ordinary Enu.

'The young man has grown to be a KONKA, the devoted slave of his URUPA. He believes he can no longer bear to be separated from the cause of his truly remarkable ordeal and

34

is prepared to take it upon himself in a most spectacular way, by building a nest on top of his hair, which is not uncommonly padded with copra, to accommodate his URUPA, this not always being easy to afford; so that one bird may be mightily spoiled by a generous rich man, while another is neglected and badly nourished by the man who has a family to feed and only limited resources.

'It is the KONKA's ambition, the guideline for his life, never to cause his bird to desert him and if this does occur (which it often does, depending on the season, war and peace, abundance and scarcity, and other factors) the KONKA will be heart-broken for a while, but will show his courage in adversity by enlarging and beautifying the empty CHAPPA, so as to woo another winged master, and in all instances will excuse and even praise the bird for deserting him and accuse and blame only himself for his shortcomings, whether because of his purse, his humour or his physical capacity. A fortunate KONKA is he whose personal URUPA remains on his head for the rest of his natural life and will faithfully guard his grave after he departs. But many KONKA live in idle hope and vain expectation. The bird will rarely remain for ever on a man's grave and die on it, as so many a canine will do for love of a master. The average URUPA will guard a man's last home until it is cajoled or courted by another worthy soul who offers it a good CHAPPA. Then it will depart.

'As to the language the birds "teach" their KONKA, there are two: the vulgar GOULGOUL for daily use and OUNGOUL, which has a rich vocabulary and is in use only by a few Enu, and consists mainly of vowels and gutturals, unlike the common language, which is made up of consonants with hardly a vowel among them.

'Their OBRA (chief or king) and the OBRABAS (close kinsmen of the OBRA) might also converse in KAUUU, which in the strict sense of the word, is no language a tall, but purely acoustics. The Enu have no written language, for which they see no need.

'The spiritual head of the nation, which nests on top of the

35

highest authority in the land is called a MUKKAH and is either a vulture, an eagle, or a dodo. It must weigh no less than twenty-four English pounds, be of sound constitution, and can be either male or female. A MUKKAH by law should be at all times hatching a Royal plumed pedigree . . .'

All this is very interesting, but.

There was no time to ponder da Silva de Goncales' description of the Enu. There was simply too much nervous excitement in the air. The noise I had heard earlier turned out not to be an aeroplane but the deafening uproar created by a flock of large birds as they heralded the King and his court, alarming the lesser birds of prey and causing their obedient servants, the loyal and law-abiding tribesmen, to stand aside and make way for the royal procession, and, in particular, warning all who might raise mutinous and insurgent voices to shut up or be crushed under the weight of the Imperial Turtle.

The mobile throne of the highest power in the land was a three-hundred-year-old sea turtle painted every colour of the rainbow, with the sad and worldly-wise eyes of an old dynasty that had carried many a supreme ruler into noisy battles and even noisier peace conferences. The monarch was a tall, fat, venerable, decorous and awe-inspiring man, definitely more man than ape, with the pulsating muscles of a Japanese wrestler and the heroic chest of a field marshal. On his head he wore no triple crown or mitre but a scabrous, nodular, knotted hair construction at least four feet high. As king and nobles halted a mere twenty feet before me, I noticed that the birds' nests of the overlord and his barons were formidable fortresses, cemented with dry dung and mud. The largest of the imperial vultures hovered a foot above the King's head to clear the air space above His Majesty, thus preventing even the smallest hummingbird from crossing its path. Then the vindictive-looking bird made its undisturbed descent on to His Majesty's CHAPPA. Once it had alighted on its perch, all the lesser vultures, eagles,

hawks and buzzards took up position on their respective KONKAS, forming a tight protective ring around their Supreme Commander-in-Chief and blinking with a hostile, malicious gaze at the rest of His Majesty's subjects. Two tall warriors armed with spears and hatchets stood to attention. The loud trumpeting of a heron rang out. The beach fell silent. Suddenly a large pebble the size of a duck's egg shot out of the King's mouth, as if fired from a slingshot, and landed right in front of my feet, which, I interpreted, was a sign to speak up first:

'Lord and Master of the Universe,' I began, but a quick glance into his eyes told me that this was not the customary form of address. 'Humble servant of your winged master,' I started once more, with one eye on the King and one on his vulture. He seemed to like this a little better and signalled me to continue with my address with a small inimical smirk. I had quickly prepared myself for such a bombastic occasion with a few flowery phrases: 'I have come from far away, Your Majesty, because I heard so much about you and your wonderful people and your glorious country. Allow a mere stranger on your shores to reside for a while among you noble savages, so that when I return to my country I may relate the many wondrous things I saw and learned here and sing your praises with unprompted rapture, affection, and sympathy for your charming, engaging and most interesting nation.'

He obviously didn't care for this kind of formal application for permission to enter his kingdom either.

'Cut the shit, you alien devil.'

'I am a genuine castaway in need of asylum, sire, but not quite sure if you understand my language . . .'

'But I hope you understand mine. I said: Cut the shit, you foreign bandit.'

'The King in my country might have put me in jail for tax evasion, that's why I had to leave,' I lied.

'I want the truth, you mongrel bastard. You seem to us an unprofitable and taxfree property, and you are most

likely a heavy liability on your country's social services, I should think.'

'All right, then I shall tell the truth,' I said, 'though I don't think you will quite understand me, but all the same.'

'Let's have it, then.'

'I left England because a fate worse than the debtors' prison or the hangman's noose awaited me at home. The unspeakable catastrophe I refer to was that of anonymity, after my life's work was picked to pieces by the vultures of our media. These fraudulent literary con-men destroyed my *Afternoon With Psyche*, a 500-page novel, by calling it "ungrammatical, incorrect, inaccurate, faulty, improper, incongruous, and abnormal", and my mode of expression and choice of words "obscure, crabbed, involved, and confused; diffused and verbose; grandiloquent, copious, exuberant, effusive, pleonastic, and long-winded, ambiguous and digressive"; in short "flatulent, frothy, feeble, tame, meagre, insipid, and poor" – every word and every insult they could find in the *Thesaurus*, dismissing with their allusive gobbledegook my genuine concern for the human predicament.'

'Not so slow, I haven't got all day. A little faster, please, to the point.'

'The point is that these literary hawks tried to annihilate me with their filthy adjectives, yet never once mentioned me by name, not even by my initials. This, Your Majesty, is my private misery. It sent me on this ill-fated trip to learn to forget and to accept being forgotten in spite of all that I have done to hew out the truth for all to read. But I didn't think you cared much for the truth.'

He didn't. Nor did he care for this yarn or for anything else I might have fabricated on the spur of the moment to hide the 'real truth' from him, which was that I really had no idea why I should have ended up in this god-forsaken dump. He either wanted to hypnotize me or make me nervous, for he glared at me with obvious suspicion and went on waiting for me to tell the 'real truth' and nothing else. But this I decided he would not understand anyway – and

38

I doubted if he would be able to follow me. I must add that I had no idea then how proficient their English actually was. An unexpected and most extraordinary example of linguistic cloning (if I may call it that).

Only later did I find out that the present ruling class of Enu (who call themselves PUKKAS) are the product of, if not immediate participants in, the remarkable events of 1937, when in the spring of that year, Peter and Evelyn Wynn-Morgan, the newly-wed socialites, crash-landed on Enu Island on their round-the-world record flight in a Hawker Siddeley. This dashing young couple belonged to a circle of high-spirited celebrities and literary paladins of London. Middleton Murry, Bertrand Russell, Maynard Keynes, etc., were their friends, and the Americans, Hemingway and Steinbeck, Faulkner and Wilson. And, of course, the Lawrences, D. H. and Frieda.

Initially it was only the speech patterns of their new idols which the native young Turks among the Enu copied with a rare over-confidence in the magic power of impressive-sounding English words. But with their acquired taste for more and more of the same English delicacies, their appetite grew and the Wynn-Morgans soon faced the growing restlessness of their permanently disgruntled but by now high-spirited entourage who had found a new language in which to express their grievances. They had brought along a copy of *Sons and Lovers*, which became the Enu's weekly literary diet. The Wynn-Morgans took it in turns to read to them. But after they had read the novel to them two dozen times, Lawrence's masterpiece suddenly disappeared (it was stolen from under Peter Wynn-Morgan's mat while he slept on top of it) only to reappear half-digested in the faeces of those most eager to learn the new language.

The disappearance and subsequent devouring of the book spelled worse to come. Fearing the effects of their disciples' starvation of their customary idiom, Peter and Evelyn taught them any English they could think of. Not just their everyday Bloomsbury, Kensington, Foreign Office and BBC English, but Cockney and North Country, Welsh and Scots dialect and the language of the Aussies and the Kiwis. They taught them all the childrens' rhymes and ditties, household words and limericks they could think of, amused them with a free rendition of *Alice in Wonderland,* and 'The Owl and the Pussycat', taught them all they knew of Irish, American and Volapuk; and provided them with a generous vocabulary of plain parade-ground obscenities. The results were astonishing even two generations later.

The Wynn-Morgans were to become the justified martyrs of their own linguistic ebullience, because, in order to enrich their vocabulary still further, the Enu reluctantly decided in the end to 'know' the handsome couple first in the flesh, and then in their reincarnation as 'Silent Companions', ultimately grilling their remains over hot ashes and stuffing them down with a gluttonous determination unequalled even among savages. This group of English speakers soon became known as the HOWYUS, bird talk for 'how are you', and took over.

One of these venerable HOWYUS, an elder statesman by the look of it, suddenly leaned forward and shouted at me in hoarse Cockney: ''Ere you 'ave them fucking foreigners again. Go back where you come from you beady-eyed fucking bastards.' Pleased with his pronunciation, happy and thrilled for the rare occasion to show how well he could express himself, the little old man chuckled and roared with laughter, but I didn't care much for his sense of humour. I had noticed the man when he came in, not just because he made his entry with the distinguished grimace of the venerable court wizard and kingmaker, and not just because he seemed older and more leathery than the rest of the nobles (he reminded me of Peter Lockwood), but mainly because of a pink crane with red wings he carried on top of his head. This fat monster of a bird, a sleek-feathered, silent, cross-beaked ogre, had caught my eye before I noted its bearer.

It regarded everything and everyone through half-shut lids, with an insolent disdain for the dimwitted and misbegotten of this world. Unshakable in its position on top of its benefactor, it leaned back into its puffed-up feathers like an old politician who has heard it all before and doesn't care a damn for what anyone says, whether in Cockney or Enu. None of the other birds, except perhaps the royal vulture, looked as pleased with itself as this big, fat, red monster. And it never opened its beak, not even once.

The blood-colour of its feathers gave its silent authority. The bird's taciturnity was matched by its so-called owner's volubility. My only defence was swift counter-attack.

'Did you call me a fucking foreigner?' I shouted. 'You cross-eyed baboon.'

'Yes,' he yelled, even louder than before, and came two steps closer. Looking right into the gaps between his teeth I had visions of losing my arm in a meat grinder. I tried not to blink.

'Go back where you bleeding well came from!' he roared. 'Get out of here! Beat it!'

The situation looked distinctly unsafe and now that he had responded to my first counter-attack, everyone in the royal court was eager to try his bit of English on me. 'Fuck off, you pissy-arsed bastard and go and suck your mother,' was about the most polite remark slung in my direction.

What disturbed me the whole time I was watching their gestures for signs of danger was my own confusion over their language. I couldn't for the life of me understand how these savages on the other side of the world could have picked up this vulgar English. Had the army been here during the war? Had they learned it from previously shipwrecked sailors? Nor did it seem to impress them in the least that I was totally at their mercy anyway, half naked, unarmed, and exhausted. In my predicament all I could do was muster my last breath and shout (which I did, so loud it made them all shut up at once). 'And fuck you, too, you bigoted bastards, you stinking arseholes, you motherfucking, cocksucking, dirty baboons. One more word out of you filthy, stupid pigs and I'll put a curse on your fuzzy heads, and then we shall see.'

41

These, I believe, were the very words that saved me.

Now the majestic wrestler on top of his turtle cracked a faint smile. He seemed to be more than pleased to hear me so defiant. My words must have convinced him that I wasn't one to be intimidated by the brute bastards at his court, whom he probably feared as much as I did. He might even have calculated that I might be useful to him in the long run, either as an ally against his own people or as an instructor in language. He was definitely kind and even cordial when he asked: 'Where are you from?'

'From Europe, sire, from England.'

'What's Europe?'

'The continent of Europe, sire, has often been portrayed as a lush lady astride a bull, female grace commanding brute terrestrial forces.'

'And England?'

'The discarded, abandoned cape of the same lady, sire, in short, an island.'

'What's an island?'

'A refuge for sea mammals, a protective cave in the currents, a safe hideaway for snails and slugs, a paradise of clipped lawns and feelings, a country of unwritten laws and an unrealistic sense of fair play. On my island English is spoken.'

'What's English?'

'The name of the language that we speak. Language comes from the Latin word "lingua" meaning "tongue"; when we wag our tongues we produce language. At the moment we are both speaking English, sire.'

'What you and I speak here I won't call "English". You are strange to me and I am a stranger to you. We speak. Let's say we speak "strange" and let's see who can speak stranger, you or I?'

'You, of course, sire.'

But of course I didn't mean that, indeed I was convinced that it was the strangeness of my language which made him listen. But then another of his blistering glares reduced me

to a small, irritating speck of dust that had settled on his eyelid. He had one of those sudden changes of mood savages and schizophrenics are known for. His voice turned ice cold. He spoke loud and clear: 'Never mind where you're from. This is no island here, but an overpopulated universe. We allow neither emigration nor immigration. We have a full house. By tomorrow morning we want you back out to sea or we shall give you the boot! That's clear.'

'Sire, I am a survivor, a castaway. Our boat has gone down. Except for a few phantoms I saw, no one came out alive. You can't do that to me, sire, you can't be serious.'

'The law says we are overpopulated and I am the law.'

'Then you'd better kill me now, sire, and get it over with. Come on then. Strike me down and finish me off.'

My courage impressed him. He chewed on another pebble while pondering his final decision. In his eyes I could only observe oriental resignation to the human suffering of which he'd seen so much. He finally fired the second pebble right across from the bodyguard to his left, and casually, with the tired tone of the immigration officer at HM Customs Shed at Dover, pronounced: 'I suppose we can occasionally make an exception by special royal decree. Nevertheless I would not expect the court ever to cite this case as a precedent at any possible future application to land uninvited foreign visitors. Permission to land has been granted for seven days without food or water. If you survive this first week you will be allowed to stay another week under the same conditions, and should you manage to be alive at the end of the second week, a further fourteen days, subject to the same restrictions, of course, will be permitted. After one month you will be allowed to work providing you are fit to work and have not become an emaciated and useless skeleton. Should you be found fit to work you will be fed. Food rationing among my slaves is strictly enforced. Theft is punishable by amputation. All severed limbs go into the pot and are shared equally. In addition to this, slaves are allowed, for their free consumption, to fatten their own dogs and cats, snakes, rats, and cock-

43

roaches in their own kitchens. After six months' ordinary labour on various projects we might find your case eligible for an extension-of-stay for a further twelve months. Now follows a vital period of learning what it is to be an Enu – we appoint you assistant executioner. Depending on how quickly you learn to master the blow and the quick chop, within another six months we would then consider you for the position of first hangman. Being on the public payroll would entitle you to certain public benefits. You would be allowed to eat the same as all my public servants: bird droppings, shit more nutritious than tinned food.

'After completing a tour of twelve months, you would be eligible for the lifting of all restrictions with regard to your freedom of movement, except for Regulation One which enlists every able-bodied resident for military service. We are constantly at war with all sorts of rebels and every man owes his life to the sacred duty of defence of the highest authority, which is me, King IT, the Forty-second.'

I decided to plead for the moment: 'Your Majesty, let's not think so far ahead, I wonder whether I shall make it for another twenty-four hours. I am thirsty and I am starved.'

Nothing seemed to please him more than my little confession of physical exhaustion. He grinned and was much more friendly now than before when I had called his barons a flock of filthy baboons.

'To be starved and thirsty is indeed a problem and I leave it to your intelligence to solve it. You don't seem to understand that all of us, the entire universe, are at war, permanently, and there is no end in sight to this war and it is only the fittest who survive it. But that's all for now. Next prisoner.'

I had heard this one before and not so long ago. Two guards pulled me up and then threw me down a few times and finally kicked me aside like a bale of straw to make way for the next case.

The lines at the back, packed with smaller tribesmen standing on tiptoe, receded and two giant Enu warriors prodded a sad-looking figure in front of them.

I could hardly believe my eyes. It was Trevor. 'Trevor,' I shouted. All those weeks on the boat and I couldn't find him, and finally gave up. And here he was. He waved a sad hand. He was in bad shape, and couldn't hold his head straight; it wobbled on top of his shoulders, as if he had lost all control over it. His hair hung down over his forehead, his eyes were bloodshot, his tongue stuck out as if rigor mortis had set in, though he was still able to stumble along on two leaden legs. He was made to bow respectfully before the King, and thrown face downwards into the sand.

'And who are you?'

'I am from England,' Trevor breathed heavily, with only a little voice left.

'I don't know this England. I asked you who you are. Do you know this man over there?'

Trevor looked at me as if he were about to pass out and whispered hardly audibly: 'Yes. Alas, yes.'

'What does "alas" mean?'

'Alas, he is a friend of mine. He dragged me here. He made me board that ship. I told him I didn't want to go. I had premonitions. I saw it happening before it happened. I knew this is how we would end. I work for a Royal Commission. I am on my way to quite a different tribe. I have things to do, only two more weeks left before I file my report. I knew I shouldn't have listened. But he drugged me and then dragged me with him. Can't you spare a drink, Your Majesty? I am passing out.' Trevor was at his best again, and I admired his cool act.

The King gestured and next thing Trevor was holding a pig's bladder above his mouth with both hands and pouring it down. It was reddish-brown and looked like a special royal home brew.

'Trevor!' I pointed to my lips which were dried up like crusty snails.

Trevor couldn't stop drinking, and neither would I have done in his position. Finally a thin trickle of the reddish-brown liquid oozed out of his nostrils, he stopped, burped

45

once and then once more, turned to me and said, with new verve in his voice:

'Have some, by all means.'

He wanted to hand me the pig's bladder, but a flunkey grabbed it from him and emptied it on the ground a few inches in front of me. Trevor threw me a look of pity and turned back towards the King, his head still shaking, more in disbelief than from physical weakness. He must have regained some of his former wit, for he called out cheerfully:

'Who are you, what are you and how are you?'

The King seemed to enjoy Trevor's fearless, unconventional demonstration of the appropriate language to use with an Enu OBRA. He pointed to his vulture and a little above it and said: 'I am OBRA IT. It's name is my name and as we have no name for it, I am called King IT the forty-second. IT is my master. My master's wish is my wish. My master's thought is my thought. Hence I am him. And I am very well, thank you, *how are you*?'

At the magic word 'HOWYU', pronounced by him overloud, the entire court and all the tribe down the line thundered 'HOWYU' like a never-ending hurrah. It echoed from the hills and sent quite a few birds sky-high, where they circled until calm was restored and they could safely return to the bunkers, hovels, homes, and huts provided by their so-called owners.

'My name is Trevor Lunt. All English except for a bit of me which is not, but never mind. Good schools, best universities, excellent army service, fabulous teaching job. Professor of Secular Religion at Oxford; fellow of this, that and the other; eternal student of human behaviour. It's all shit. And that's what I am, Your Majesty, all shit. A nothing, a nobody. Less than that. A mere speck of an invisible atomic particle, if that. Nothing, nihil, nada, nichts.'

'Keep talking, Mr Lunt. Tell me more.'

'Please consider my presence as an optical illusion. I am not here. Or rather I shouldn't be here. I can't be here. It's not possible. I am on my way to the Makkundas of Paasch Island, but I made a mistake and didn't listen to my more intelligent self. I am the most stupid, most idiotic, most . . .'

'That's enough. I like what you said but enough. Lunch for Mr Lunt,' commanded the King.

How they did it I'll never know, but within a minute or so a hot meal was conjured up and served in a pumpkin bowl. It smelled of succulent roast pork, delicious fried rice, and chicken pineapple with cashew nuts and ginger. Kneeling there he began to wolf it down. Crawling over to him on my knees, I opened my mouth wide, saliva foaming down the corners. Trevor turned around and amid much hilarity, occasionally tossed a cube of meat or a sliver of pineapple into my mouth, but when he tried to feed me properly, two men held him down, and two others grasped my arms behind my back, so I couldn't reach out for those pitiful crumbs. All I could do was to stretch my neck as close to his hand as I could get it and keep my mouth wide open. Then Trevor burped once more and gestured that they should give me the leftovers, which they did in their own savage way, by pouring them in the sand right in front of my nose so that I could smell but not touch the food.

Every time my head went down, they allowed it to come slowly closer, but then, with one sharp pull, jerked it back. Small pigs shot out from under the many legs, and within seconds even the good smells had vanished with the pigs, who left nothing behind but their excrement.

Trevor had drunk and eaten enough for the week, and after these special favours, expected, rightly I thought, to get even more concessions out of the old bastard.

'I wonder what happened to your ships, Your Majesty. I need a boat and can't see a sign of any boat here. Did your ancestors burn them so they would never be able to cross back to the normal world?'

'What normal world?'

'The other one, Your Majesty. The world that we, he and I, come from and where you should and could live as well.

If you get me this boat, Majesty, I shall get you something you'd love more than a boat.'

'What could that be?'

'Reason, Your Majesty. Reason plus imagination. A powerful combination.'

'Do I need that?' He sounded offended.

'Of course not.'

'So why offer me something I don't need?'

'Because that's all anyone can offer you. With a little imagination, even you will realize that there is no reason for you to remain so isolated from the mainstream of our civilization. Reason will help you understand that you may remain as savage as you please in concert with the rest of ordinary humanity, and that there is no need for you to close yourself off. Certainly no longer, now you have been discovered. You look to me like a man, not an ape. It's men, not apes, who build ships, who sail the seas, who despatch messengers and missionaries, astronauts and satellites to explore the horizons, navigate the cosmos, walk on planets, discover new galaxies.'

'Discover what and why?'

'Discover that no man is an island unto himself, discover that the family of man is one big happy family dedicated to the common good of all. That's what you have to discover, too. Expand, Your Majesty, stretch yourself, get out of this province, this backwater. And why? Because expansion is man's objective, the purpose of his existence, the alpha and omega of his innermost drive. Man's life should be one voyage of discovery, exploration of the unknown and unmapped inner spaces, as our friend Dr Tony Mang would say. While man is exploring the universe, he is actually discovering himself, I would suggest.'

'Do you really believe all this bullshit?'

'No, of course not. But it's my job to make the Royal Commission, in whose employ I travel, believe that I believe in it. All I really want to do is protect you from intruders, defend your independence against foreign invaders. Remember, it is

48

discover or be discovered! Conquer or be conquered. Invade or be invaded. But for us to take you along we need a boat.'

'We Enu mustn't touch sea water or anything that touches sea water. We therefore don't know how to make boats, if we ever did.'

'Then allow me a tree trunk to build our own boat.'

'All in good time. I shall consider it. First comes the law. First come our "Restrictions for Immigrants and Temporary Visitors". First of all let's have a try-out of two weeks without food or water, followed by two more weeks of the same; should you survive the first two. After a month, we might use you in the Army Engineering Corps, building bridges and tunnels, and that kind of thing. We need all the brains we can get. Nowadays there are no brains. God knows where they are. We are fighting a losing battle against the DUPA. You look as if you'd never heard of them, a tribe of belligerent females occupying HOSA, the highest peak in the country. From their inaccessible bases in the mountain crevices, these female monsters raid our farms, abduct our men and children, kill our cattle, destroy military outposts, knife and strangle all male travellers, and make all our journeys unsafe.'

'How many DUPA are there?'

'Two or three LAKHS.'

'How much is a LAKH?'

'Either one or two-hundred thousand, I'm not sure.'

'How many inhabitants has your country, counting both friends and enemies?'

'Half a LAKH, I should think.'

'How can there be two or three LAKHS of rebels when the total population is less than a quarter of it?'

'How? I don't know. Facts speak for themselves. The country is in a mess.'

'If you feed us, both of us, we'll help you against all the DUPA, but not on empty stomachs, sire.'

I thought Trevor was doing fairly well without my help, but all the same, I wanted to add that he shouldn't hesitate to tell the King that, like anyone else who has a mouth full

49

of theories, we would, of course, when it came to it, help him in every way and in every war. (We were not pacifists, either of us.) And tell him that we believe in wars that can be won. The trouble with the war he's fighting is its unpredictable outcome. Hence it should be avoided at all costs. Tell him that too.

The King must have been reading my mind when he addressed Trevor: 'Mr Lunt. Before you decide to go out and kill DUPA in exchange for your daily ration of meat and rice, I suggest you reconsider the wisdom of our decree. During your quarantine on the beach you will have ample time to ponder the horrors of war that you'd face the day I let you out of confinement. The way we kill here, with claws and teeth, might not, I fear, be to your taste. We Enu rejected war machines and ballistic missiles quite some time ago. We believe in looking our victims straight in the eye before we strangle them and we are taught how to face the enemy without blinking an eyelid. Now that we no longer wage wars between men, but only against the female of our species except for the fucking HURRU, those petty bastards – may God remove them from this universe, we pray, because we ourselves don't seem able to get rid of them – eye contact has become the sole method of engaging the enemy. At times our fighting will seem like a lover's embrace until you look again and notice how one of the two parties is slowly expiring from his or her wounds – and this is not speaking metaphorically.'

'But, Your Majesty, you might also lose both of us within fourteen days. You might even lose your war.'

'Frankly, Mr Lunt, winning a war brings new problems we might not be able to face. If we lose, we lose. Many a loser becomes the ultimate victor. If this sounds decadent, it is nevertheless the wise meditation of our sages. Anyway, we don't need you right now. Next prisoner. Hurry up.' He clapped his hands.

Trevor was pulled by his hair and thrown to his knees, kicked in the groin and backside, and landed in the sand next to me. He threw up his delicious lunch only two feet away from me. The small grunting scavengers arrived again from all directions and carried off this meal as well.

One evening on board ship before the troubles had begun, at the end of one of the interminable ballroom parties, I had walked out on deck with a stout, handsome young woman named Bella Karpakos and talked to her about stars and waves, thinking all the time of a smiling retreat to my cabin after captivating her with promises and charms. As we watched the shoals of silvery flying fish, she told me her dream was to marry an intelligent man of independent means. She had relegated her need for physical love to the level of the engine rooms far below deck, where a number of stokers and electricians shared her luscious body either one by one or collectively whenever she asked for that kind of attention. She had also told me she had been around the world for the second time now and felt she was getting closer to her ideal man, who must certainly be intelligent, even if he had no means of support, her mother having bequeathed her a house on Naxos, and her father and brother (both killed in Cyprus by Turkish terrorists) having left her a factory in Kentish Town which produced plastic handbags. She had sold the factory and had rented her house on Naxos to German tourists and was thus quite well off financially, but at the age of thirty-five no longer satisfied with her unmarried status.

On board ship Bella had never been seen without very expensive silks and golden costume jewellery, her hair sprayed and perfumed and neatly arranged in a beehive which was fastened with pins and combs by the ship's hairdresser.

Again, as at Trevor's entry – the circle of spectators opened up, as if by magic hand. And the same two guards who had pushed Trevor in, now accompanied Bella with solemn, haughty looks befitting the occasion.

Poor Bella looked pitiful in her torn nightgown, unable to conceal all those exposed parts I had wanted to share with the crew in the engine room. Her hair, though it was partly dry by now, hung about her head in a hundred ringlets, and

51

she looked like a veritable Medusa who had just stepped out of the sea. If anything, I found her more attractive than before. She seemed fairly cheerful as she stood before the King, waved a hand and called over to me: 'Hi! Good to see you! Where have you been?'

The Enu customarily shave their pubic hair, both men and women. So far as I could judge from their grimaces, Bella's lush growth unsettled the natives. I began to realize why the Enu shave their pubic hair. Sex organs unframed by hair are like the organs of small infants. Unarousing. Evidently the birds saw in Bella's lush bush a cosy ready-made nest and went for it. Each time a bird flew at her, Bella hit out but missed them more often than not, amidst bouts of hilarity. The King and all his barons chuckled with laughter.

'What brings you here?' laughed the King.

'My name is Bella Karpakos. I, too, wonder what brought me here. I still can't tell but I suppose it's you, Your Majesty. I came all the way from Kentish Town, London, England, to take you home to my family, sir. Aunt Elena likes my men to be weird, strong, and powerful, and she'll definitely take to you. I'd rather bring you back home, sir, than anyone else I've met so far on this terrible cruise. But, thank God, that's over and here I am. At your command, Your Majesty.'

She spread her arms, waggled her tits and belly like a belly-dancer, stuck out her tongue, rolled her eyes and when she finally felt she was getting enough attention with her act, she turned around and showed the King and court both halves of her most convincing argument. Appreciative noises like 'O, o, o,' conflicted with the glazed look the King gave her. To judge by his expression he had never seen anything like it in his life before. She certainly impressed me with her uninhibited performance.

When the Enu mind goes blank and can make no decision, unlike us they can depend on their feathered super-egos to make up their minds within seconds on their behalf. Suddenly a large, fierce-looking black crow lifted itself from the three-foot turret of a big and handsome savage in his mid-fifties (who looked to me, judging by the solemn expression he was wearing, the embodiment of court morals and manners), and made straight for Bella's eyes. Now the unbelievable happened. Bella, faster than anyone would have imagined, hit out at the bird, while simultaneously lifting her right leg and bending her torso sideways. This happened so fast that the cry of 'Koko, Koko!' which was either the name of the bird or that of his half-bemused owner, was drowned by the heart-rending screech of a mortally wounded bird. When Bella straightened up on her legs, the bird had vanished and all that could be seen of it was a few black feathers at Bella's feet. Pleased with herself, Bella grinned, waved and called another 'Hi!' in our direction. The King, though stunned by what had just transpired, didn't lose his cool manner.

'What next?' he wondered out loud.

'What next indeed,' Bella shouted back. 'It's an outrage. I demand compensation. The fucker could have blinded me, had I been a little slower. But thanks to my hockey . . .'

The rest of her words drowned in a carillon of shrill and angry voices. Koko was gone, where, no one could imagine, but he was definitely gone. Now Koko's alter ego came at Bella with fists and uncut toenails. 'Slut, cunt, trollop,' he yelled, and probably would have murdered her. The situation didn't look too good for her. There was a little pause, it only lasted seconds but long enough to produce yet another unbelievable trick. Bella suddenly bent forward, reached down between her legs, removed a big wet bundle of feathers, plunked it right back on Koko's headgear, where it fluttered for a few breathless moments in its last mortal agony, lifted its head once more, opened its beak, shut its eyes, and expired.

The riot was only minutes away. The utterly horrified and confused crowd would have lynched Bella, and probably Trevor and me as well, but for the quick action of their Chief, who would not have been King of the Enu and held sway without his iron fists and his bloody mind.

'Koko,' he demanded, in a stern voice. The man whose

bird had just been destroyed, still shaking all over, stepped before his Overlord, who grabbed him instantly by the neck and choked him to death with his left hand. Koko's body slumped down next to that of his bird.

In the ensuing silence the King said firmly: 'That is for allowing an alien female demon to destroy your better self. Enu be warned! The hand of your Monarch is made of steel.'

Justice meted out with a public display of no-nonsense authoritarianism does the trick. Most of the Enu went down on their knees and some prostrated themselves on their faces before the Hand Made of Steel. It was obvious that the King had no intention of allowing a trivial incident to grow into a general riot, which could end in revolt. Bella was treated just like Trevor and me (except for a few more kicks on her backside than they had given us, which she took with equanimity), and ended up in the sand next to Trevor. To prevent the wild hogs from devouring Koko and his feathered Master, more or less in front of his grieving relatives, half a dozen servants sprang forward suddenly, cleared away the bodies, smoothed the sand with palm fronds, and returned to their places.

'Next!' I heard the King shout, impatient with all these Greek antics. I knew that for every new survivor they produced our ordeal would be extended. That any one of us should come out of this hell alive to tell the tale seemed impossible.

Next was Tibor, the Hungarian waiter from the Gay Hussar in Greek Street, Soho, who, after thirty-five years, was on his second honeymoon with his second English wife, Sylvia Pearl, a quiet innocuous woman from Highgate with the gentle manner of a drunken pigeon. Tibor was built like a boxer and didn't show his sixty years except in his grey receding hairline. He had spent half his life in London, and this was his first trip out of the country. He had the large handlebar moustache of the legendary Magyar horseman, the proverbial ladykiller who reeks of Barac in the morning and Tokay at night, and marries so as to get a free hand in acquiring an entire harem, in silent accommodation between Pasha and first wife. While Sylvia would sip endless martinis in the saloon, with a crowd of cardplaying ladies from Torquay, Tibor would be the first after and before dinner at the Beau Brummel Bar on the top deck. He was the man with the loud laugh and the perennial jokes about Hungarians and Englishmen – all of them filthy. When Tibor used to enter the Beau Brummel he would let fly with: 'Long live the Hungarian revolution!' which always cracked a smile on the faces of retired chartered accountants who were bored with their constant boozing and chasing skirt.

Now standing upright before the King, his trousers dangling from braces, a heavy silver cross over his shortsleeved vest, which he had somehow managed to salvage, he looked the film star he probably dreamed he could be. The same horsey grin, the same self-confident manner. On his right wrist he wore his golden wrist watch on a golden metal strap, which was Tibor's major conversation piece when he was not discussing genitals. To my great surprise he had saved this as well. This gold watch was a little larger than ordinary watches, octagonal and covered with knobs, dials, colours, and buttons to press. It immediately caught the King's attention.

'What's that thing on your wrist?'

Tibor twisted and turned at the ends of his moustache. He was obviously thinking of a witty answer and unfortunately for him he thought he had found it. He was trying to charm a dragon who had both a cynical sense of humour and hands made of steel. I regretted Tibor's misjudgement of this savage ogre and pitied his foolish attempt to sell a tall story to an Emperor used to dealing with liars and cheats, maniacs and necromancers in his own court. I had tried it and ended up chewing my dry tongue. Trevor did the same and was equally maltreated, because, in fact, he had no Royal Commission to report to, but was trying to escape a marital predicament and whatever he had managed to keep down for a while he had to throw up when they dumped him next to me.

Tibor's ingratiating Hungarian tactics began promisingly

55

enough. 'This instrument, Your Majesty, can tell you where you are in time and space. Ha ha ha.'

He more or less repeated word for word what used to be his standard joke at the Beau Brummel, but in the King he had found a match for his trivial jokes. The King took him literally, something none of us would have ever done.

'This whatever it is will reveal to me where I am and what time it is for me?'

'Correct, Your Majesty. I can give you your personal location in time and space.'

'By looking at your hand instead of mine?'

'Yes, sir.'

'Then tell me where I am exactly.'

Tibor pretended to scan the horizon, looked at his watch, and at the clouds once more, then at his watch, and pronounced solemnly what no wise soothsayer would ever dare whisper in front of a tyrant as paranoic as King IT.

'Very soon you will fight your last battle, a battle over life and death.'

'I will?'

'A battle you will lose.'

'I've never lost one.'

'The enemy will destroy you and dump you into the sea, or a rebellion will break out and your prime minister will bury you up to your neck in an antheap. This watch is set only to tell the truth and nothing but the truth, so help me Our Lord Jesus.'

Though by his own standards he was very funny he had no inkling of what savage humour is really like.

'Hand over the watch,' the King suddenly bellowed. The unexpected outburst of royal anger caused something of a panic and many thin legs began shaking as if the wind were blowing through the undergrowth and a dozen or so faint-hearted tribesmen promptly disappeared into the bush. Every arm and leg was on the move. Tibor, stood there erect and defiant, and refused to hand over the watch.

A second command by the King would probably have

created total bedlam among his subjects. To prevent it, a tall warrior stepped forward, held a wide machete and grabbed Tibor's arm ready to bring down the steel. For a few seconds Tibor kept everyone in suspense. He shouted defiantly: 'Nishta!' which I took to be Hungarian for 'Never', but by some unforeseen grace some sense must have returned to him. He quickly removed his cherished talisman and threw it up to the King. The imperial vulture caught it and would have gobbled it up but the King reached quickly above his head, squeezed the bird's neck lightly, and the watch fell into his lap. He inspected it closely, shook it in cupped palms, banged it on his shin until its glass splintered into a thousand pieces, ripped out its various hands and dials, looked into its entrails, saw something he couldn't quite grasp, and with two jabs of his left forefinger claw (he wore claws over thumb and forefinger of both hands) he had within seconds turned a perfectly good wrist watch, waterproof at that, into a small heap of tiny wheels, springs, and other diminutive metal parts which he then wiped from his knee with the gesture of someone who had spilled food over his best and only pair of trousers.

The King in his turn had, sphynx-like, forecast our doom, by looking into the entrails of Tibor's timepiece. Things looked grim for all of us, but for Tibor the destruction of the watch was something of a personal tragedy. The watch had been his one and only friend, and had won him status wherever he showed it. He had saved it from Cook's henchmen and now his pride, his jewel, gone, like dust to dust, he behaved like a man gone berserk. He fell to his knees, produced genuine tears, sobbed, whimpered and cried, shouted 'Maria, Joseph, Mama, Brother and Christus,' lifted his arms and prayed (in Hungarian) for his own death and a speedy delivery from these ghoulish creatures who had nothing better to do than eliminate his last item of identity just for the sport of it.

'Vandal bastards,' he groaned through clenched teeth. 'May the stuffed prick of a horse rupture your mother's

57

filthy cunt,' he cursed the King, in a free translation from his native Hungarian. But neither King nor court seemed impressed by his histrionics. Several of the nobles turned their backs on him and farted trumpets in his direction. The King, too, broke wind so loudly and forcibly as to cause a three hundred-year-old turtle to shake on its hindlegs.

The end of Tibor's watch spelled the end of his virility. The arms on the dial mingled in his mind with the many outstretched arms of lonely female travellers in the first, second and tourist classes. His charm had been ruined, his amulet was a shambles. His ultimate reason for existence was torn to shreds. Tibor was not unaware of his heroic posture as he stood on the brink of total defeat. He wiped his tears, pulled himself up, protruded his chest, stamped his feet, drummed on his rib cage, and roared once or twice. A captured gorilla realizing that the gate had been shut and locked before his very face. In short, he practically went mad.

The Enu must have had their own long experience with psychotics. They certainly impressed me with the swift application of a local version of EST. A hardly audible whistle. Two medicine men (recognizable by the blue feathers stuck in their anuses) came rushing into the circle, followed by two younger assistants pulling at the ringed nostrils of a buffalo, an unbelievable, prehistoric monster, all black unkempt carpet and large, wild bloodshot eyes. Trained for this special purpose the buffalo charged at its target, and then stopped dead in its tracks. Another whispered command and the animal swung around and drenched the delirious, convulsing Tibor with several gallons of sharp-smelling urine, delivered with uncanny precision right in the centre of his face. That did it. (What a splendid demonstration of native technique in the handling of psychotics!) It worked. Tibor began first to smile, then to laugh and ultimately roared with laughter as they kicked him in our approximate direction. He lay there, eyes turned upward, bellowing with laughter, for a good ten minutes until he fell quiet, dead to all further convulsions of his mutilated ego.

'Next one,' snapped the King, 'and this time a little faster.'

Next in line was Herbert Burk Humpelman, Burk for short, Professor of Philosophy at the University of Chicago, who had been the most unpopular passenger on board. None of us at the Beau Brummel Bar had ever been able to make out what an American egghead was doing among ordinary people from Woking, Surbiton, Bromley, Brixton, Belfast, and Newcastle, who had lived out their whole lives and never seen a single volume of either Proust or Schopenhauer, and were travelling round the world in search of more fun, sex and alcohol than they were used to at home. People who never ask questions and never dispute learned propositions and whose sole existential *angst* is the end of the cruise and having to go back to office, supermarket or workbench.

That one might never come back at all probably never occurred to any of the passengers, except to Burk, who at every opportunity tried to engage people in several outlandish topics, such as Wittgenstein's *Tractatus* and Spencer-Brown's *Mathematics*. To judge by his permanently sour expression, only 'the American' (as we called him) might have foreseen the events of the night when we crossed the dateline and lost the ship. The man behind the clay pigeon shooting stand and the sozzled ladies at their cardtables would greet Burk respectfully to his face with a cheerful 'Good morning,' and whisper, 'there goes the American nut' behind his back. Burk didn't mind and was always on the move. And always alone. In his search for someone to discuss Sartre's *Nausea* with, he tramped many miles a day across decks and lobbies, restaurants and games rooms. I had only met him once. One Sunday, the very first out at sea, after lunch, on the Captain's bridge. A pleasant warm sunny afternoon made for harmless jokes, mindless puns and sun-bathing. We were all having what's called 'good clean British fun' when Burk, without any provocation, began to explain to John Hodensack, First Lieutenant, and a few other officers, who at first believed he was pulling their legs, that the terms 'latitude' and 'longitude' should properly speaking be interchangeable, depending upon which way you looked at the globe. Clearly a totally silly argument which no one felt like taking seriously but Burk, who had the TV robot voice of a Dalek, which was always good for a laugh. When the conversation did not take the turn Burk had intended, he suddenly swung around and brusquely walked away, a greying Boy Scout with pink-coloured cheeks.

The way Burk Humpelman glanced at us now, I could see he would have been happier had he been the sole survivor. The idea of having to spend time with us bored and depressed him. He tried his best to ignore us.

He looked at the King with utter revulsion and to judge by the monarch's face, a mutually shared nausea was all that these two men had in common.

'And what's your fucking name, you miserable midget?' The King sounded harsher, more impatient.

Burk replied in his husky Dalek voice without looking at the King but also without any trepidation: 'I was christened Herbert Burk. Surname is Humpelman. Probably German or Pennsylvania Dutch. What does it matter? I am who I am and that's all there is to it. Frankly, I couldn't care less who you are. For a moment I thought you might be Caliban, but then again, you might also be Prospero. We certainly didn't stop here because of a tempest. Nor do I have the slightest idea where we are. It's another dimension, for sure, but it's not that unfamiliar. I feel like I've been here before, I feel I'm back in my own old schizophrenic nightmare. Surrealist scenery, mysterious catastrophe. Some big insurance fraud is my guess. Alas, those who planted the explosives overdid it and blew themselves up. The wrath of the gods? Nonsense! A slight human error and it happens. Happens all the time. As far as I'm concerned, keep me here or throw me back into the sea, it's your problem, not mine. One glance at you tells me you can't possibly be more savage than we are and we are no more savage than you. All this regalia around you seems a bit silly, and is more or less useless I should think. Why bother? We do the same, in the States. A lot of decoration and no real essence is the style of our White House. Stupid custom and ceremony. That's all. Anyway I am tired and would like to sleep. Now make it quick, sir, I'm not interested in arguing with you. Anything you say, sir.'

Neither their fierce looks nor their spectacular birds seemed to impress Burk Humpelman in the least. The King was not used to this kind of abruptness and was obviously intrigued with Burk Humpelman's talk. He glared at him and had a puzzled look in his large brown eyes. To seem more relaxed, he picked some remaining scraps of food from between his hideous teeth, spat what he found into his right hand, and kneaded it into a small ball between thumb and forefinger.

'Your profession?'

'Philosopy, which is actually no profession, not even an art, but a kind of passion, if I may say so, a love affair with knowledge and wisdom. I am not sure which. I really don't know. What ultimately matters is not what you know or why you know what you know, but what you feel you ought to know. Do I make myself clear? Philosophy actually is no science at all, though some idiots call it that. Nor is it a history of the intellectual elite, as Semmelbaum (I don't think you know who that is) calls it. Charles Spencer-Brown puts it better: philosophy, he says, is a man's lifeblood spilled among the pigs. Anyway what does it matter what it is? You won't understand anyway. Nor do I wish to enlighten you, come to think of it. Right now I want to sleep. And in any case, you wouldn't grasp what I had to say, your IQ can't be very high. Freud says man is as neurotic as he is primitive, and the neurotic has a low IQ. That's a fact. God knows, maybe analysis would help you, and make you a happier savage. A romantic idea. The French would love it. Makes no difference to me. I can see you don't care either. That's good. But now, enough of that. Where can I lie down?'

'Would you consider the recently vacated position of court

astrologer? Our previous soothsayer lost his right and then his left eye by using too much salt.'

'Sir, I don't quite understand what you are getting at.'

'Then let me explain. Our late friend, the astrologer royal, developed the unfortunate habit of forecasting unpleasant events. We subsequently rubbed salt in his eyes to stimulate his optical nerves, this being our conventional cure for glaucoma and cataracts. Bad vision reflects bad eyesight. And visionaries should try to retain excellent vision. But the salt didn't do him the usual good. After he lost both his eyes we lost the man because the poor bugger committed suicide!'

'Don't make me laugh. Suicide, here? In this dump? I don't believe you. You probably bumped him off. Anyway, appoint me to whatever you like. You can't scare me with your suicide story. Astrologer or zoologist. I am at your service. I've seen suicide attempts. Failures and successes. Suicide is a desperate way for a man to prove dramatically the old existential truth – that life isn't worth it. As long as you don't insist I share a hut with my former fellow travellers, I'm your man.'

'You may sleep while you fast, Mr Burk. Fourteen days no food, no water. But . . . you might also not make it, not enough of that!' (He slapped his bulging stomach.)

'Thank you, thank you, sir. May I go to sleep now?'

'You certainly may.'

The King motioned to one of his flunkies with feet the size of short cross-country skis and with a single well-placed kick, Burk tumbled next to Tibor, rubbed his back with one hand, put the other under his right ear, drew his legs up into a philosophical question mark, and dozed off despite the bedlam that accompanied the arrival of Sylvia.

Sylvia seemed as if in physical and mental agony and was followed by a platoon of yelling and dancing warriors. Her mind was obviously clouded by foot-long pink and red penises and disturbed by the clicking noises the Enus' balls make every time they hit the pelvis. It was the clicking she couldn't quite place (she later confided). It baffled her and she was afraid that there was something wrong inside her own belly. When she noticed her husband Tibor, his head buried in the sand, she seemed somewhat relieved, she wouldn't have liked him to see her now, in her present lamentable state. She smiled at everyone with glazed eyes, at the King, his courtiers, and at us. Sylvia, for many years a virtuous woman, was no longer naive. Recent experience had taught her that all men were savages, not just Tibor and his drunken friends, as she'd always thought. The King, probably relieved to hear his last case of the day, had a sudden change of mood again and even displayed a silken charm when he addressed himself not only to Sylvia, but to all of us:

'I don't expect you to acknowledge that it is we, not you, who are sorely tried by your unexpected arrival. We may well be savages and primitives in your eyes, but we have our own ideas of civilization, and our ideas happen to coincide with the highest values of all civilized people within our known universe. As far as we can judge you, you seem to be enemy aliens from somewhere in the outer regions of our galaxy, and we don't know who or what you are. While I am talking to you our astronomers are investigating the approximate location of your settlements among the stars. We shall not know the results for a while. Meanwhile we consider that we are dealing here with unidentified aborigines, I hope you appreciate that.

'Most of the things you say, even though we understand the words, are hardly comprehensible to normal human perception. Are you quite sure you are human? All I can say is: you invaded us, whether voluntarily or not, and now you say you wish to remain here. But we do not touch sea water, nor do we live in proximity to any creature emerging from the sea. We neither fish the ocean, nor do we build ships. We believe that nothing good ever came from it. As I said before: the only way to render your presence harmless to us is to purify your bodies of unknown substances. If you can't survive without food and water we shall conclude that your bodies were too putrefied and you might well infect all of us. We are not heartless apes, as you may think, but pragmatic men. Our primary interest is the wellbeing of our species, and nothing else. I suppose that's normal. Should you survive the next few weeks, which I doubt, we may well arrive at some amicable agreement; and as for you, my lady, we recommend you hold yourself in readiness for the requirements of my soldiers. What is your name?'

'Sylvia Pearl, Your Majesty. Married to the big fat slob over there, but I love him, Your Majesty, I love him with all my heart, and all I beg of you is to let me look after him. He'll need all my help. If you'd only allow me a little coconut milk, I might have the strength to get by. If you want me to I'll sleep with anyone who fancies me. It doesn't mean that much to me you know, that's the way we were brought up in Winchester. My first duty is to help that poor silly creature of a husband.'

'You shall be allowed the milk of twenty coconuts, once a week. This special grace and favour is in exchange for your services, the exchange to take place at the far end of your permitted territory. You seem to be an honest woman, of uneasy virtue and not too bright. My men love that.'

'Thank you very much for your kindness, sire. It's awfully nice of you. Thank you ever so much.'

She would have thrown herself at the feet of the King to cover him with a thousand little kisses had he not shown her his teeth. He then addressed all of us again.

'From the bay on your right to the sea oak and the lagoon on your left is your territory. Everywhere else, and except for this woman, is out of bounds. Don't any one of you dare venture near the tree line or you will be instantly annihilated. That's all for today. I must be off.'

'Fall in! Turn! By the left, stand at ease – attention!'

'Goodbye Your Majesty, goodbye,' Sylvia waved and shouted.

With vultures flying ahead and buzzards closing the ranks at the rear, the King, followed by his entourage, began his

64

road back. Turning an aged turtle around through ninety degrees seemed to be an endlessly slow process. It took quite some time for all the King's men to find their places in the ranks according to standing, position, influence, privilege and special merits. A colourful crowd followed after them, walking twenty abreast. At last they were on the move, slowly at first, their feet trudging over the hot yellow waves of sand, and ultimately they vanished into the green of the interior, leaving little else behind them but a thousand small red circles on my retina. They were gone. I looked at Trevor and Bella, Burk and Sylvia lying there before me in the sand, like a family of seals washed ashore by a freak wave, and I saw the beach, empty and deserted with nothing in the sand, not even footprints, nothing but the excrement of pigs and Enu, which was soon carried off by a flock of black and white ravens. I thought for a moment I might just have woken up.

Three

Once time and location can no longer be determined, reality soon fades out like a distant voice on a remote radio station. Past and future intertwine and yesterday's event turns into a memory of idle expectations; what is left is neither future nor past but an all-embracing present. And even now, long after my return, I still relive this present as if it were taking place now.

This present reality disturbs all my sceptical faculty and I simply lack the imagination to invent this kind of thing. Result: I believe everything is true and there is no other reality. Fortunately (or perhaps not) I am not alone in my predicament. There are these five other people, very much alive; they are real people who have real stories and families just like my own. Yet (strangely perhaps) we do not exchange this kind of information. We don't discuss our past. We don't believe it makes sense to talk about events and people that are as remote from us as the dead are from the living. Burk, in fact, believes we have crossed the river Styx and are in another world where we should expect to find Arcadia, island of the blessed, but have run aground on the reefs of a remote purgatory, and are probably heading for a blazing hell. (Burk proved to be wrong. We ended in paradise, a Garden of Eden of sorts, but this none of us could have foreseen.)

Meanwhile we look round. The sea is as calm as on the first day after creation. As far as the eye can see the land is covered with thick jungle. To the East and North high

66

chains of mountains lie across the blue skies. The Southern perspective is flat and barren – one feels the ocean extends from here all the way to the South Pole. There is no wind, not even a slight breeze. The days are hot, unbearably hot. The white sands cannot be crossed once the sun stands high. We walk slowly when we have to, but preferably not at all, and spend most of the day in small trenches we have dug for ourselves with our bare hands. Anything that crawls or creeps we catch. We remove heads, stings and legs and eat the rest as if they were locusts. A small yellowish brown beetle half an inch long called a *koro* tastes of plain garbage. Trevor, who is instructive about such things, has seen them before and claims the *koro* constitute the staple diet of a little-known pygmy tribe called the Luala who inhabit the rocky shores of North-Western Samoa. The main art of eating *koro* is to keep them down; their taste is rotten and so is their smell.

An *aga* looks like a cross between an ordinary cockroach and a bedbug, lives in vast colonies like a termite and constructs clever traps for sea turtles who cannot right themselves once they tumble on their backs. In less than two hours the *aga* will devour a hundred-pound turtle leaving nothing behind but a bare shell. While they are at work on this these carnivorous pests fortunately make a sound like crickets. If one hears them it's wise to move on. We remove their sharp fangs, heads and legs and eat them before they can get us. Alas, every mouthful seems to taste worse than the last and causes a rash on the wrists and ankles. They affect me like amphetamines and make me nervous and itchy.

A *murro* has a round head, the size of a marble with no eyes in it. Its colour is blue and red. Instead of eyes this small creature sports a minute elephant's trunk through which it 'sees' the sandflies that it picks up with quick jerky movements. *Murros* are fun to watch. They leap about like ordinary fleas, except that their size prevents them from attaining the same speed, which makes it easy to catch

67

them. They taste of strong game but, according to Trevor, they contain all the vitamins and minerals the body needs. After one has gobbled down half a dozen or so of them one's fingers and toes go numb for a few hours.

Even more nourishing but also more revolting in taste are the *tongo*, the turtle eggs containing half-formed embryos. A few bites and you instantly feel you are losing all sensations, and your brain is paralysed. You enter a padded cell, a not altogether unpleasant experience which may last all night long.

The nights are cool. Thick mist covers the waters. Behind the lace curtain of this milky white fog or mist shooting stars or other heavenly bodies cause silvery fountains to cascade upwards. A weird spectacle of shadows, white on white. Every time one of these meteors hits the water the ground trembles, and the sea rushes up the beach for a few moments but soon rolls back, as if it were mercury.

There is no reason to stay here, none except holding on to a last chance of being discovered. We still have a faint hope. Naval vessels searching for lost top secret missiles. submarines patrolling these southern latitudes, even the odd fishing boat could come along. Anything might happen as long as we stay out in the open, visible from afar. Once we enter the green thicket we'll never be seen again. Meanwhile we are being observed. Thousands of eyes are focused on us. God knows how many Enu watch every single one of our moves. We pretend we are unaware, but as the days pass we become more and more conscious of those eyes. We are naked ghosts covered with sores and small festering wounds. Breathing is painful and speaking is almost out of the question. Why waste our breath? What is there to be said? Our efforts at digging for fresh water are rewarded for a few brief moments. The water quickly seeps away and we have to dig again and again. Sometimes we fall asleep in the midst of our work and wake up believing that all of our reality is a bad dream. Then one early dawn something very strange happens which changes our situation radically.

68

From the direction of the bay to the south comes a howl,
part laugh and part whinny: it comes closer but we seem
too limp to move a muscle. Trevor shrieks: 'Sorels!' and
though none of us knows who or what a sorel* is we leap
from our trenches like hares and race towards the lagoon
which lies to the north. A herd of sorels closes in on us.
Their breath is putrid. They smell of rancid blubber. They
have the bodies of seals but human eyes, ears, mouths,
noses and lips. Human tongues try to form words. They
cannot speak, they gurgle. They waddle along and scold us
for running away. They are shouting something but we
don't understand what. It is clear they mean no harm. Later
we learn that they are totally harmless but in constant need
of human company and will chase for many miles after a

* Sorels are an aquatic hybrid between Australoid aboriginals and seals
and are so named after their creator Auguste Anatole Sorel, the French
society doctor, also called 'the French Rasputin', who was born in
Grenoble in 1829 and died 'somewhere in French Oceania' in 1905.
In 1862 Sorel was banished from Paris and sent into exile for practising
Black Magic with some of his patients, which had caused a scandal when
an elderly sister of Napoleon III died of a heart attack after returning
from one of Sorel's 'secret sessions' at his country house in Neuilly. The
maître of the 'Société des Magiciens', undisputed master of necromancers supreme, was sent into a gilded exile and given an annual
allowance of six thousand *louis d'or* by the state, to do his research in a
new branch of medicine called 'human engineering'. With the blessing of
a great number of those notorious intellectual charlatans Paris was (and
still is) teeming with, Sorel started his First Oceanic Laboratory for
Genetic Research on 29th April 1865 on a small atoll off the coast of
Tahiti. He seems to have had inexhaustible funds at his disposal and
made a point of sending monthly 'letters of progress' to his friends at
the Academy of Science, who made sure Sorel's name would not vanish
from the pages of *Le Figaro*, *L'Aurore* and many scientific publications.
For a few feverish months the Paris press was alerted to an impending
breakthrough by the genetic genius, Professor Sorel – and a number of
journalists set sail from Toulouse to be in at the christening of the 'new
man' Sorel had promised in time for Christmas 1866. Journalists and
scientific observers came from as far as Boston, Massachusetts, and Rio de
Janeiro but by the time they arrived in Tasmania to take the boat to
Tahiti, Sorel's experiments had turned into a genetic nightmare and he
refused to receive anyone who came to pry into his business. Three
hard-nosed American correspondents who had bribed their way to
within less than a mile of his laboratories were assigned by Sorel to

lone hunter, who may very well mistake them for seals and kill them.

They are hollering and shouting something that sounds like ''Alt, 'alt', but our nerves are too frayed for this new encounter and, without giving it a second thought, we dive into the lagoon to escape them. We have hardly crossed over when hordes of Enu rise from trenches, climb down trees and step out of the jungle, like a living wall of alligators which have been simulating death until their prey comes within easy reach of their jaws. Within seconds an entire army of painted warriors surrounds us. We stay frozen.

They circle us. A loud clatter of teeth. They are so close we can smell them. Rotten wheat, mouldy straw. They keep a small distance away from us, not quite sure whether our

---

'special duties', which consisted in arousing two-year-old seals for his insemination experiments on the fourteen-year-old aboriginal girls Sorel had bought from their parents under the pretext of sending them to France for higher education. The girls had to kneel bottoms up. Sorel and his assistants would smear them with the secretions of female seals on heat, and while the bulls roared with passion, Sorel would grab their pricks and manoeuvre them into the vaginas of the poor little girls who usually passed out at the very first contact with one of these giant sea-mammals, which can easily crush one of their own species beneath their mass of blubber. Later reports stated that more than two hundred little aboriginal girls lost their lives to Sorel's madness. And they were not the only victims. Some of the bulls turned violent, which happened not infrequently after contracting shankar and syphilis from their human partners, and Sorel had to shoot them. Sorel's story belongs in the text books of every student of contemporary history. He was a pioneer with the utopian vision of a coming master race which could be bred under laboratory conditions. He died a victim of his own obsessions on 5th May 1905, crushed under a six-hundred pound ogre of a seal, whom he had nicknamed 'Goliath' and kept as a pet and bodyguard for over six months.

The creator died but his creations mysteriously survived him. Some of the bulls had succeeded in impregnating native girls who then gave birth to armless and legless creatures with an oily brown and black hide but with the eyes, ears, noses, mouths, lips, teeth and tongues of humans. These hybrids, later called 'sorels', simply waddled away from their mothers and swam out into the sea never to be seen or heard of again – yet they probably inspired Karel Capek in his War with the Newts, as he might by chance have sighted them on a journey to the South Pacific shortly before World War I.

species, when encircled, stings, bites or scratches. Suddenly they turn their backs on us, as if about to leave, but this is only a manoeuvre. All it takes is for one of us to shift his weight from one leg to another and they instantly swing round with right arms lifted and left legs thrust forward, ready to attack. Then they turn their backs again and this they repeat a few times. It is obviously an ancient ritual, to show us and the sorels, who stand yapping on the other side of the lagoon, that they are firmly in control of the situation.

The sorels shout something in unison. It sounds like ''yena'. Are they calling the Enu 'hyenas'? Their voices grow louder. They make gestures, as if they are about to enter the lagoon, and cross over to get at them and at us. Then follows the loudest laughter I have ever heard; it seems to rise from one huge mouth. The Enu laugh but then suddenly growl and snarl. The sorels, too, make aggressive noises. Any moment now I expect them to be at each other's throats like two packs of wild dogs. Nothing of this kind happens. The shouting cools their anger. Voices gradually quieten down. Standing high on their tails, the sorels wave at us with their pathetic flippers, turn about and waddle off.

With all this going on I hadn't been paying attention to the huge fowls on top of the officers or to their smaller brethren – assorted finches, sparrows and robins – hopping about on the heads of the lower ranks. There is something both sensible and natural about classifying men according to the kind of birds they carry. One tends to forget a man's face and concentrates on the bird on top of his head instead.

A large black eagle with a few neck feathers missing gives us a filthy stare. He rolls himself on his belly on top of a feisty Enu who looks to me like a man of certain standing. Then the eagle gets to its feet, spreads its wings majestically and in the process hits out at other wings. Now all the other high-ranking birds unfold their wings in a splendid performance worthy of the best number in a Chinese circus.

The Enu beneath the black eagle opens his mouth and I can't believe my eyes at first but there it is. The man has double rows of teeth and this monstrous mouth can speak and, what is more, speak in a familiar idiom.

'Where the 'ell do you lads think you are off to?' pronounced in a broad Cockney, was not the kind of opening line we had expected.

We all stammer the word 'sorel' and shudder just to think of them.

'They're fuckin' scared of us, can't yer see for yerselves!' Colonel Black Eagle chuckles and slaps his belly.

As if by command the other officers do the same. They all laugh and slap their bellies.

'When we get 'old of 'em we grab 'em by the balls and shake 'em, like that!' He grabs one of his fellow officers amid loud laughter to demonstrate his point. 'But quite honestly, lads, we'd rather have nothin' to do with 'em. They stink like meat gone off.'

We couldn't but approve of his last observation. Even half an hour after the sorels had departed the air seemed still putrefied by their particularly unpleasant odour.

'You skimpy creeps, on the other 'and, seem not to care one way or another. Well, good for you. We was waitin' for you, as you well know.'

'What's going to happen to us now?' Bella managed to shout, trembling all over. ' "Don't you do 'em any 'arm, Colonel," was his last instruction before the old bugger went back for his royal nap. "I want to see them strange fuckers once more before I do 'em in my own sweet way." '

'The old fucker is going to do you in his own sweet way, that's what's going to happen, madam, and that goes for all of you. Any of you ever been on a buffalo?'

A short whistle and out of nowhere appear half a dozen shaggy old buffaloes with extraordinarily long legs. It later turns out to be a special breed of these powerful humped oxen, exclusively bred for army transport. Their legs are as tall as the legs of camels and, as with camels, it is quite a performance to see them go down on their knees. It doesn't take the Enu long to tie us with many tight knots against the hard and high backs of the riding saddles which are made either of leather or wood. I notice the officers sit on small cushions but this is considered too much of a luxury for us. When the animals finally move, it feels like riding on top of a tank with both its chains missing. This doesn't help us to keep our last supper of insects down and we all become violently ill to begin with. Fortunately we are tied on firmly or we might easily have fallen off and cracked a few ribs. Starved and hallucinating as we are, nothing seems to hurt us any longer. Though sick and tortured we are somewhat relieved that the King has not ordered his men to kill us instantly, as he promised he would once we left the shore.

The train is endless. Officers both ride ahead and cover the rear. On either side we are guarded by three fierce warriors who hold bamboo sticks to prod us with when we doze off and slump forward. The heat is unbearable and I think my brain has shrunk to the size of a walnut. We finally reach elevated terrain after passing through dense jungle. Unexpectedly the entire train comes to a halt. The guards share their water skins with us to prevent us from fainting. Black Eagle suddenly appears and delivers a little speech of which I remember only the gist, which is that we should pull ourselves together so we don't look like poor sods deserving pity but rather display the faces of the mean bastards we probably are at heart. 'Look grim, or there is going to be trouble.'

We try our best to look grim and hide our feeling of relief at having escaped the hell of the seashore.

Gradually we reach a plateau. The air has cooled off dramatically. The shore lies miles below to the west. We are heading north-east and will have to climb even higher. A light breeze starts up and we begin to feel alive again.

Did the trek take fourteen days, as Trevor later claimed, or only six hours? I cannot tell. I recall steep winding roads which lead higher into the mountains and along a narrow river which runs noisily over a bed strewn with boulders of all sizes, a sparkling mountain stream cutting many corners and rushing forward and downhill, while our path leads up into quite different vegetation. I have seen similar landscapes in the wilder parts of the Tirol and in the Pyrenees. Suddenly there are fruit trees on both sides of our path and the air is filled with the sweet scent of jasmine and orange blossom.

'We shall soon be in G'NAAUU, our capital,' says the guard to my right, proud and pleased with himself at getting this one sentence out. I look at him. A strange transfiguration has taken place with the change of climate, proving convincingly that the human face, as we know it, needs a human climate. The unbelievable has been happening in front of our very eyes. Snouts have divided themselves into separate noses and mouths, teeth seem to have retracted, the gaps between them closed. Ears have shrunk, eyes have taken on the ordinary expression of fatigued men. The air is light and even crisp as on the peaks of high mountains.

'G'NAAUU means paradise,' says my guard. A glint of hope has returned to our eyes, not because we expect to enter paradise shortly, but because of the air which can be inhaled with full lungs. Over the roofs and ramparts of G'NAAUU, which is built on top of several small hills, circle low-flying formations of long-necked giant condors. Occasionally a bird dives down and returns, its beak holding a struggling human body which then vanishes gradually down a bulging, feathered neck.

Closer to the walls of the city the forest ends abruptly. Golden fields of rye and wheat extend all the way to the walls. Swarms of Enu crowd the ramparts and gates. Our colonel exhorts us once more to look firm, fierce and defiant, so no one should feel in the least sorry for us. He puts on a sour face for us to copy. Then he commands his men to pass round a goat hide containing a milky liquid. It tastes of orange-flavoured tequila and makes one feel instantly awake and aggressive.

I feel as if an alarm had gone off. Here I am, a prisoner in

74

a strange land at the mercy of a most curious tribe of aborigines who speak minimal English well enough to enable them all to pass the Oxford Proficiency Test with grades of 'good', 'very good' or 'excellent'.

Even if this should later turn out to be hallucination, one thing I am certain of: I am not sitting at my portable Smith-Corona electric in London making it up.

The gates of the city are thirty feet high, carved in red teak and guarded by two giant turtles, of which it is hard to tell whether they are alive or stuffed. Walls and ramparts are of grey quartz boulders. An indestructible bulwark of a medieval fortified town. As we enter through the gates a shout goes up and makes many a bird fly up in horror. It is the long drawn out 'U' of the by now familiar greeting of 'HOWYU!', the never-ending howl all Enu utter when they welcome a stranger.

We are no ordinary strangers but stranger than any creature they ever set eyes on. In successive waves the throngs move forward and back, clap, laugh, scream and stamp their feet. They pull faces at us and shout 'GUIGUI', which is a nickname for pets. Many just stand there with mouths wide open, too flabbergasted to utter as much as a sound. These are the more sophisticated and sensitive souls. The others are simply out of their minds with excitement and obviously gripped by a messianic fever. We are their Martians and our arrival evidently heralds all sorts of forebodings. To save ourselves we now try our best to look like the mean bastards the colonel advised us to pose as. It keeps most of them at a distance, though not all thousands of them. Hands reach out to touch us and, but for our guards and the tall soldiers specially trained in crowd control, we might have been crushed to death by their enthusiasm and sheer curiosity. The guards punch the noses, box the ears and hit the bellies of those who are too forward. Hardest to control are the thousands of young men who simply jump on to the backs of the elderly and crippled for a better view. The latter's screams of agony mix with the happy shouts of joy in a vocal orchestration such as I've never heard before and would not know how to describe. And then imagine that above all this bedlam thousands and hundreds of thousands of birds of all colours, shapes and plumage hover and flutter, drone, hoot, chirp, twitter and coo but are mainly occupied in gorging themselves on the holiday's special offerings which are called 'LOOLO'.* These offerings they return more or less immediately so that the city and its citizens are covered with a thick layer of birdshit and feathers and smell accordingly. This is no ordinary city, we soon realize, but the world's biggest aviary. The houses are arranged in clusters and shaped like eggs. The windows are oval and so are the balconies, doors and entradas. In fact, there are no straight lines anywhere to be seen – all is eggshaped, oval, in this phantasmagoric chicken coop called 'paradise'.

We are finally allowed to dismount and stretch and scratch ourselves before the gates of our prison, a fine building standing in its own grounds, the colour and shape of a giant stuffed tomato. Most of the other houses are painted in various colours like Easter eggs, except for the Royal Palace and seat of the Government across the huge oval-shaped square, which looks like an orange-yellow pumpkin. The king and all his advisors are out on the many balconies to

---

*LOOLO is the word for 'special offering'. The birds' excrements are called FUYU (Holy Shit). From FUYU the government in its own factories produces a sort of Royal Jelly called BOTO. A few drops of this oily elixir of life added to water can cause a man to rise from his deathbed and allows women to deliver painlessly. Strong stuff. All FUYU belongs to the state, except what falls on your person or your private property. The expense of making BOTO is too great for the ordinary citizen, who normally sells his bit of FUYU to the state, whereupon he receives an advance of BOTO proportionate to the amount of FUYU he has traded in. No money changes hands. The health of the country, which is based on the acquisition and distribution of this ultimate source of human energy, is thus wisely entrusted to the birds, whose wisdom the Enu rate higher than their own perverted intelligence. I would certainly like to interest serious bidders in the few samples of BOTO I brought back. The results of a first brief chemical analysis carried out at the Allan Laboratories at Watford and of tests made for curative properties in the treatment of arthritis in fieldmice were definitely positive.

make sure we are locked away safely. Our trial is still to come. When it comes it will be quite different from what one might expect in the present circumstances. But meanwhile we embark on a comfortable life of smug satisfaction to have got this far.

We are not allowed to put a foot outside (not that we desire this kind of adventure) but are free to roam through all the hundreds of oval-shaped rooms (not all painted crimson, but some vermilion, ochre and yellow). We soon find out that this prison was until recently inhabited by royal retainers, who have moved out their belongings but not their servants. We are surrounded by an army of willing and helpful hands. Some of them slaves, others servants and others again call themselves 'guards'. There is not that much to do for us, for reasons I will explain later. There is hardly any work for the slaves. We are left to our own devices and can do as we wish. The first few weeks we spend scouting the place out and we are always finding new chambers tucked away in odd corners, some of them inhabited by families who have hardly taken notice of the fact that their former masters have moved elsewhere. It seems to make no difference to them.

There are innumerable staircases connecting a web of passages. Some are slim and frail, ascending like mystical spirals, while others are broad and grand, solemn, like temple steps. Staircases everywhere like an Esscher labyrinth. They lead to gardens on various roofs, to verandahs and to an inner courtyard which is amply furnished with alcoves and niches, figurines and benches and other fine examples of ornamented masonry. At the centre of this yard a fountain shoots water seven feet in the air and around it are neat beds planted with hibiscus and lilies. The dream of a nineteenth-century trader from Portuguese East Africa come true. The main entrance to the mansion is from the north, from the Royal Square, and all the windows on the northern façade over-look this square and the variously-coloured egg-shaped buildings which house the country's élite. There are two more entrances: one to the east for servants only and one to the west for official visitors only. The southern side faces an uninterrupted vista across miles of rugged landscape and affords a perfect view of the volcano called HOSA which is surrounded by snow-topped mountains.

But let me give you a better picture of the world we live in. By way of the northern gateway (also carved in teak), one enters a wide coaching entrance shaped like an arch which leads to the kitchens. Above these there are many rooms, but to reach them one would have to go through the courtyard, turn right and walk up some stairs. The kitchens are open to the comings and goings of visitors and a stream of servants unloading the produce that feeds our vast establishment. Through the western gate one enters the ceremonial reception rooms via three 'gothic' arches. The rooms themselves are scantily furnished with low tables and hollowed-out wooden egg-shaped chairs. The seats for the guests of honour stand a few inches taller than those of the hosts, so as to give the guests a sense of their own importance. The walls of the reception rooms are decorated with many bas-reliefs of hunting parties, reminiscent of early Illyrian art. The floors are of white marble and red onyx. Compared to the frugality of all the other quarters these reception rooms seem opulent.

Each of us occupies three or four rooms in different parts of the mansion. The walls are white but tinted crimson, pink or vermilion, and make you think of a Greek Orthodox monastery in Ethiopia. The original tenant for whom this house was built obviously cherished the ancient tradition of contrasting exterior pomp with interior modesty. The entire place is in remarkably good taste but the architectural masterpieces of the edifice are undoubtedly its toilets, splendidly decorated like Hindu shrines.

At first we are simply impressed and more than a little puzzled that so much effort should be spent to beautify this humble place of privacy. On our first arrival, when the King said we would one day be eating the same as the rest of his people, i.e. shit, we had thought that this was his ordinary vulgar way of talking and took no further notice of it. When we sat down to our first meal in the city and everything tasted extraordinarily delicious it never occurred to us that the food we were eating might, in fact, be POK, the local recycled bread. Should we have been suspicious right away when we saw daily deliveries of fresh meats, dairy produce, fruit, vegetables and cheeses with not one misshapen carrot and not a single worm-eaten apple among the lot? Should the brilliant colours and the fresh, wholesome smell have made us wonder how in the world could they grow such fabulous fare?

Like so many revolutionary inventions, POK was discovered by a combination of accident, economic necessity and simple ingenuity. It happened in the wake of a government commission to survey the 'economic profitability of traditional methods of waste disposal'. The commission stumbled upon a pungent truth if ever there was one: that waste, so called 'night soil', here called POUP, which was usually ploughed under or fed to the pigs, was being wasted. Fertilized or not, all soil still requires rain. Good harvests depend on good weather conditions, which cannot be relied on. An outbreak of swine fever may easily destroy within a few days or weeks the fruit of years of hard labour rearing pigs. More important still: statistics showed a seventeen per cent annual increase in human waste production and a mere four point two per cent increase in population. Less people were clearly producing more shit. An untenable situation. Were the present trend to continue, the commission warned, the entire population might soon be swallowed up in its own waste, as in a quicksand.

Psychiatrists tried to explain the phenomenon with reference to 'a recently increased infantile neurotic activity which is triggered off by manifest oedipal aggressions directed against the parent-child bond; a volatile expression of pent-up violence inseparable from peace-time frustrations under

79

authoritarian rule' and more of this kind of incomprehensible OUNGOUL.

The government concluded that the economists who had warned that all of G'NAAUU would soon drown in its own waste sounded more convincing. From now on, waiting for rain and hoping for healthy pigs were to be considered 'reactionary' thinking. The people's demand for lower food prices and better quality with more variety inspired the Enu engineering élite and served as an eye-opener to many an experimental scientist. And, as in a true revelation, a horn of plenty was seen to be clogging the metropolitan sewers and seriously blocking the progress of 'advanced modern society', as the Enu liked to call their democratic monarchy. Chemical engineers were called in to help solve the problem and came up with the only authentic solution ever applied to this universal enigma.

To their credit, it must be said that the Enu, unlike ourselves, pass laws through both their houses of parliament within days and sometimes within hours. A bill for the Protection of Human Waste to the benefit of the entire nation, and for the effective punishment of thieves and speculators, was passed unanimously and became law at once. A totally revolutionary concept of nutrition, later to be known as POK ('recycled bread') was immediately launched on a massive scale. The process of recycling was to be carried out in four basic stages, known as The Four Basic Doctrines of Survival:

1. The POUP (also referred to as 'ultimate matter') is to be treated at 2000°C in order to deodorize and detoxify the substance to begin with.

2. The new odourless POK is to be reshaped and remodelled to resemble the original items completely.

3. Fibre, texture and substance is to be returned to the POK item appropriate to its shape.

4. Four hundred or more different artificial colours, flavours and odours, plus massive doses of vitamins A, B and C to be added to the final product.

The result is nothing short of miraculous. POK turned out

to be cheaper by half than the original, and its price was gradually going down, thanks to over-production of raw materials. Moreover, it cannot be distinguished visually from the original and, above all, it is generally agreed that POK tastes better. It can also, without reservation, be marketed as pure organic food to those who constantly worry about nutritional values. This outstanding revolution in food production, which caused prices to spiral down and not up, naturally transformed the economy and with it the entire society. Starvation and famine, endemic malnutrition and rickets and other diseases and the social upheavals that go with this kind of plague, instantly became a thing of the past. The effect on the street scene was dramatic. No longer would emaciated ghosts emerge from the shadows holding out bony fingers towards passers-by, as we still see them do from São Paolo to New York and from Bombay to Birmingham. Soon the streets were full of obese monsters, outsized wobbling figures, weighing hundreds of kilos each.

Of course it was not all plain sailing to begin with. The initial campaign ran into teething troubles, as many traditionally minded Enu refused to eat what they had been taught for generations to regard as taboo; but gradually reason triumphed over prejudice and the tastes of the masses defeated the epicurism of the élite, as you might expect. 'Eat More Natural POK!' was the slogan in those first years. The eating of recycled food shifted all national priorities, of course. Working and paying taxes, so that a man might feed his family and the state might have the means to keep its institutions going, also became a thing of the past. The citizen's new supreme patriotic duty was to attend to his natural functions once or twice a day. When we arrived, this private personal effort for the benefit of the entire nation could still be carried out in the seclusion of beautifully ornamented toilets among flowers, candles and burning incense. But rumour had it that new facilities were to be erected, the size of a football stadium, for a massive public demonstration of patriotism, to be called POUPOLYMPICS or 'national shit-ins', featuring teams, champions and heroes, from the fattest man of the year producing the biggest turds to a dwarf with golf ball-sized droppings.

In all fairness it must be stated that the POK solution solved all other pressing problems except one, but we shall come to that. The basic needs of the masses were now taken care of and once this happens the incentive to work for a living ceases. Leisure is simply called 'boredom' and to be bored is considered not only shameful but also unhealthy. The previous generation had still worked for its living; the present one searches constantly for any kind of occupation and is willing to pay its last fingerprint for a job.* To be occupied is everyone's ambition but hardly anyone's good fortune and the masses look just as disgruntled and miserable as in our major cities. While in Europe and the US the unemployed are still a small minority, according to the latest available Enu-statistics about ninety-eight per cent of G'NAAUU's population is either permanently unemployed or only partly employed, which makes this paradise of consumerism a triste abode, swarming with sullen and sad citizens.

Another major source of work amongst us, the exercise of reading and writing, is totally absent. There are no offices. A written language does not exist. No one ever remembers a time when letters were put down in writing, though I met with scholars and philosophers who claimed that the Enu used to know the art. There are plenty of quills, of course, but neither ink nor paper. Yet without the means to read or write and finding little else to occupy us, we rapidly develop all the syndromes of lifers. Following Trevor's instructions we have tried to make paper from copra fibres and birch bark. Trevor claims to have watched the natives on Celebes making their own paper in this way. They boil equal parts of

* The Enu monetary system, just like our own, evolved from stones to gold and paper and finally to fingerprints. Every Enu male is allowed a hundred thousand fingerprints for his life's necessities. For all practical purposes the terms 'buying' and 'selling', 'paying' and 'getting paid' continued to be used.

bark and fibres together with human or animal bones to bind the pulp. We worked at it every single morning for many weeks, but in the end we had to give up. We had produced cauldrons full of a gunky mess which, when pressed under heavy stones, simply fell apart.

Four

Our relationship with our 'guards' is complicated by semantics, as most of them speak no English and have never heard the word 'no', which does not exist in their local languages. This relationship also depends on whether or not we let them work for us. Every hour we are busy is an hour when six of them sit around, swatting flies and looking miserable. They plainly resent seeing us work. One would expect prisoners to be forced to work but not here. Physical labour, a high status symbol, is reserved for an élite who can pay for it. This club of mandarins, much like our own unions, jealously guard their jobs for close members of their extensive families, because physical labour is the only labour that keeps the body fit.

Idleness equals punishment. To be prevented from working and to lack the freedom to find something to do is the worst fate which can be meted out to a condemned man. Where but in a prison can one be forced to be totally idle? To be prohibited from doing anything at all all day long is both torture and punishment. We are not even allowed to wash ourselves but have to put up with four 'washers', who take ages to do their job thoroughly. Afterwards come the inspections by 'cosmetic supervisors', who survey every inch of our bodies to make sure the 'washers' have done their work properly. After each inspection come the 'controllers' who force sticks wrapped in cotton wool down our eardrums and up our nostrils.

Fortunately for us the various bonds of friendship and

kinship among our guards cause feuds and intrigues. We can exploit their quarrels if we are quick and then we can put in half an hour watering the flowers while they decide among themselves whose turn it is to open the tap. With all this going on the air is thick with tension and hostility. One morning Bella spilled some milk and insisted on cleaning it up herself. Immediately six servants went down on their knees to lick up the milk and it practically came to blows between us and them. But at the very last moment, to avert a major disaster, Boa, our prison governor, called in a government emergency labour relations consultant.

All these consultants are called PAKO and ours, a fairly pleasant Enu in his early thirties, brought a winning smile and a no-nonsense attitude to his difficult task of sorting out who is allowed to do what and when.

According to this PAKO, the agony of boredom justifies neither aggressive behaviour nor the withdrawal symptoms of deep depression. He calls everything an 'activity'. Looking at things is called 'action' and the same is true of being observed. Listening in silence is considered an effort no less worthy than speaking. Our PAKO interprets all frustrations as ambitions which lack economic motivation. People not guided by strictly materialistic aims are bound to fight about principles and dogmas. He has obviously never heard of Karl Marx. His mentor might have been Konrad Lorenz (although he knows nothing of him either) because he believes all social activity is a result of the genetically conditioned feeding movements which people will perform, whether or not they can gather anything in this way. He was relieved to learn that where we come from we have more or less the same situation. Our post-World War II generation, I told him, lives in a comfortable nest of consumerism but is constantly dissatisfied with the material achievements of the last thirty-odd years. We, too, fight about dogmas and principles now and no longer for mere survival. We name our principles: 'socialist' and 'capitalist', 'fascist' and 'democratic', but ultimately we use bullets and dynamite to make our point. In addition, we have the magic power of the written word which kills people by the million. I could hardly expect the PAKO to understand how a mere few typewritten pages called the *Wannsee Rapport* could have destroyed more lives between 1942 and 1945 than all the plagues of the European Middle Ages put together. How can one make this clear to someone who has never seen written words? How can anyone believe that a pamphlet, or a book, or a few sheets of newspaper are capable of sending a man to Vorkuta, into exile, into a lunatic asylum or simply into his grave? Try writing 'My Motherland is a whore and we are all sons of whores' in countries as different in their social systems as Russia or the Argentine, Iran or Libya, South Africa or Cambodia and see what happens. In the United States a man who writes a letter threatening to kill the president goes to jail. All words are dangerous, of course, but written words are more explosive than dynamite. Words such as 'communism' and 'capitalism' are murderous. Words like 'Catholic' and 'Protestant', 'Jew' or 'Muslim' are as powerful as a ground-to-air missile. A misunderstanding of written terms may, if used correctly, cause war and instant disaster. Because of printed instructions we may all end up dead before the century is over. It's the mind that sentences a man to death, certainly; but it is respect for the written word that executes the sentence. Whether we call America 'communist' or 'capitalist' or the Soviet Union 'fascist' or 'socialist' actually makes not the slightest difference, except to those who get hurt while writing and publishing the wrong thing. Most of history is the recorded and unrecorded story of plain stupidity. We are supposed to be creating a world fit for ordinary human beings to live and breathe in. Instead we are gradually choking to death on verbs and nouns – if not on air pollution.

I explain to the PAKO that we, too, build elaborate machines, designed to afford us more and more leisure and that fortunately no one in our world calls leisure 'boredom'. Not yet, although this too may soon be the case. I also explain that, alongside the socialists and capitalists, we have maniacs who call themselves 'anarchists' and 'nihilists' and are out for blood, for the sport of it. They are the children of those people who, having lost their strength initially fighting the Nazis, ended up drinking some of their blood. This new generation is now content with a new nationalist and socialist system. How else shall we explain our contemporary nationalistic and socialist tendencies all rolled into one with racialism and bigotry – as we currently find them in South Africa and Argentina, in Cambodia and Chile, in Czechoslovakia, in Cuba and many African and Asian countries. Just like under Hitler, we can have more or less full employment as long as we keep making arms. The bigger and smaller countries compete, just like cartels and corporations, in selling them to anyone willing to pay for them. The working classes, just like under Hitler, cynically collaborate with the warmongering politicians, while all the time complaining that there is neither enough work for them to do nor enough reward. The Third Reich lasted twelve years but this Fourth Reich has been going on for more than thirty years now and is based on the same laws of brutality, falsehood and infamy as the previous one. We are half way down a spiritual cul-de-sac and once more preparing undreamed-of disasters and that's the way it is where I come from, right now at the beginning of the eighties and no cheap food will help us there. Perhaps eating people instead of our shit might alter our conditions dramatically.

To change the subject, the PAKO brags about the Enus' great architectural achievements, like their subterranean factories and the underground old people's homes to which all citizens over the age of eighty are confined, to save the trouble of burying them later. I tell him that we too lock up our old people, but so far mainly above ground. The chimneys of our factories and refineries are also above ground in order to pollute the air. Yet notwithstanding the increased pollution there is also a healthy increase in the world's birth rate, which may well persuade us to think that pollution might be good for us after all. As far as our own impressive cathedrals, pyramids, skyscrapers and other large buildings are concerned, these are traditionally erected for pagan worship, because most of us feel duly humbled in front of mountains of stone erected on an inhuman scale. These gigantic artefacts are an expression of our fears. We now feel more and not less miniscule in the vastness of space and it is possibly our theory of an ever-expanding universe that has fostered an unconscious desire for self-annihilation. In order to achieve harmony with the universe we expend our energy in striving to become smaller and less significant until we are ultimately reduced to the size of an atom. How else can I explain our obsession which creates thousands more nuclear weapons annually, while the combined nuclear arsenal of the US and Russia alone already suffices to wipe out the entire world population thirty-five times over? Why are we hypnotized by a nuclear doom? Because we are too big for our boots. That's why we are afraid to challenge the gods. On the one hand we say we don't believe in the apocalypse yet on the other hand we spend billions building shelters hundreds of feet below the Rockies, the Alps and the Urals so there may be enough survivors to mourn and envy the dead.

The PAKO is unimpressed by my doomsday predictions and looks at me as if I were either too naive or too dimwitted to grasp facts. He addresses me as if I were a minor or a slightly backward or very neurotic teenager to whom the truth needs to be broken gently.

'Believe it or not, we went through all that. We had our nuclear cataclysm and survived it very well, as you can see. Our story of the creation tells us that once upon a time our ancestors, afraid their nuclear arsenal might blow up by accident, gathered all the nuclear bombs together in one place and put a match to them. The subsequent explosion created yet another black hole in space, a vast crater, but, as you can see for yourself, there are plenty of us who survived on its rim and we neither mourn nor envy the dead. If you think all this is too fantastic, too unbelievable, and that you are hallucinating, remember we do exist. This is proof in itself that a nuclear disaster does not harm those who are prepared for change, not just a change of mind but a change of body as well. The divine spark of perpetual survival is part of man's genetic make-up, say our sages. We are mutants. For mutants we don't look too bad, do we?'

'No, not too bad at all and I wish we, too, had some of your divine spark in us, but our stupidity has ruined everything and certainly our spirits. Whatever remains of them has been bottled. We live in junkyards filled with dead wires burnt out by good intentions; abandoned generators of pious wishes; rusty dynamos of progressive liberal nineteenth-century ideas. In other words our intellectual powerhouses are kaputt and we are finished.'

'Would you call yourself a pessimist then?'

'What is that? I am a moralist, like all writers. Can't you tell?'

The PAKO's task is not to distinguish moralists from cynics: his job is to help us prisoners to accept the inescapable logic which tells us there can be no exit from our present reality, which Burk has christened, in French, 'La Grande Machine de la Merde'.

Of course we could stay here at government expense for ever and will probably be kept as well as zoo animals, which, considering the present cost of living in London and New York, might not be the worst of all possible worlds. But, however convenient that might be, if there is a way out from here we should take it. I, for one, am ready to go back to London.

Before leaving he asks: 'Excuse me but what is a moralist?'

'Someone who cares,' I hear myself say.

'And a writer?'

'Some people say a writer is a person who finds the words and has the courage to write what he thinks. I think a writer is someone who locks himself up with his typewriter, pens and paper and ruins his health because he believes his craft and his ideas are needed. A writer is someone who hates himself and loves the world. In short, a madman of sorts.'

I then suggest to him that the authorities should either try us as soon as possible or allow us to build our own boat, because, if nothing else, constructing a boat would certainly keep us busy for quite a while. Should we manage to make it back to where we come from, I promise to return as soon as possible with planeloads of TV sets and other electronic gear which is simple to handle. I also promise him that we shall tell the world about them and many countries will send their pictures via satellite. TV culture is guaranteed to abolish boredom for at least two more generations of illiterates.

He has, of course, no idea what a TV set could be and when I tell him: 'It is a box in which pictures appear and disappear when you press a button,' he becomes even more confused.

He promises to put in a good word on our behalf at the Ministry of Defence. They might not give us permission to build ships, not knowing what a ship looks like, but as a new war is being prepared against the DUPA, the GUKO and the HURRU – a large scale war this time (I should treat this information as confidential, of course) and all new wars usually guarantee full employment – our chances of getting down to work soon are now better than ever.

'Once more,' he says, 'Excuse my ignorance, sir. I understand what a writer is, I mean to say I know what the word "writer" means. It means someone who writes – whatever that means. My question, to be more precise, is: a writer of what?'

'First of all, if I may say so, you do not know what a writer is; you have never drawn a figure of speech on paper. Secondly, you can't grasp what it is to read these symbols back. You'll only know what it is when you can do it. Thirdly, even if you know how to spell and construct sentences, the way others construct houses, you still need to make a house that's not just comfortable to live in but also a place you like, a repose that never bores, a home from which you can look out and feel safe being inside. You have to know *why* you write what you write, even if you don't *know* you know it; or, to put it differently, you have to construct a place for good spirits to dwell in; or, to put it differently again, you have to be inspired by good spirits, who supply you with words to express what can basically not be expressed; in other words, writing is the art of those who cannot talk. You ask me: "a writer of what?", meaning *what* do I write? But I am trying to persuade you that there is no *what*, no purpose to this exercise. There is no point in talking either, for that matter.'

'You mean you actually don't wish to tell me *what* you write.'

'I wish I could. The truth is I don't know. Writing is not a profound activity, and yet that is exactly what all non-writers want it to be. They hear the word *writer* and what they really want to hear is a message, something prophetic, something ordinary non-writing people may or may not believe when they see it in black and white. But I am talking to the wrong ears.'

'Far from it, sir, you are not. I would like to know why I should learn reading and writing, which some of our wise men recommend and others condemn – none of them practising themselves what they term "the noble art". Why should a man read what you or anyone else writes?'

'It makes a big difference whom you read, my dear sir. If you read Anouilh, for instance, you know the world is slightly off balance, particularly when the bourgeois cloak of respectability covers it. If you read Ionesco you believe the world is made of stage props and is a stage and nothing that appears to be real is ever what you think it is. If you read Beckett you learn that despair is a pleasant evening out at the theatre. And if you read my plays you know that there is no despair either on stage or off. There is simply no theatre at all unless the printed word moves people about. On stage and off.'

'What exactly do you mean? My OUNGOUL is better than my English.'

'Then let me tell you in confidence, sir, whether in OUN-

GOUL or English: literature is made by hard work and not by scholars. It's not made by critics, nor by reviewers, nor even by an appreciative readership. Literature is made by the sweat of the brow, by outcasts from paradise. Can you name me any other labour of love which no one needs and no one wants to start with except the individual who performs it? Such labour is like an offering to a deity. Writers are psalmists. Will that do?'

'Psalmists. Yes. But what praise are you singing, praising what and whom?'

'Let's leave it for now, sir PAKO. I have to get on with what I am doing which is going back to my hammock and dreaming.'

He left and I returned to my hammock to mull things over. Though bizarre, our predicament is real. Why doubt this? Was the *Katherine Medici* not a real ship? Did she not really go down with all on board, except for us, a few very real survivors? All and everything is real. That's a fact. Yet – there is something utterly fantastic in meeting an entire people who have survived a nuclear holocaust. Our own survival after a shipwreck seems fairly banal by comparison. Have we landed on one of America's testing grounds in southern Micronesia? The natives of Bikini and Enewatak were taken off their islands before the Americans tried their new nuclear devices.

But not the Enu. They were either not made to move or simply forgotten or (and this is also not unlikely) they really are a tough breed of a newer and even braver race than an Aldous Huxley could have anticipated. Remarkable people!

Daydreaming in my hammock, I think (as so often in recent weeks) that within the dimensions my brain operates in, my presence here, though real, is nonetheless totally incomprehensible. Again I experience this vacuum just a few inches above my head. This empty space of unknowing. It suddenly occurs to me that the Enu may well have a point in filling the spaces above their heads with birds to watch, listen and talk to. The interesting electronic devices I have been promising suddenly seem prosaic gadgets when compared with the birds and the poetic love of the Enu for them.

Not having much else to do and only for the fun of it, I place crumbs of bread and meat on my hair to attract my favourite birds, the CARROCKS (a cross between a canary and a parrot, a small yellow bird fluent in four local dialects and an accomplished singer). The CARROCKS come, a little distrustful first, flutter cautiously over me, only gradually losing their fear, and land on my head, grab the crumbs out of my hair and make off. True, I do not make a serious effort to retain them, but even this half-hearted attempt to attract birds to sit on my head, if only for a few minutes, is adequate proof that I am about to lose my mind. I console myself that I am not alone in this. The events of the past few months have affected us all and by the time we have to face the court none of us might be judged mentally fit to stand trial. Comparing myself to the others, I feel, in fact, that I am better off than the lot of them.

Burk has spent the last month or so imitating the movements, looks and cries of an owl, sitting mostly on his haunches and hooting away through the night. My little game with the CARROCKS has been child's play by comparison. Burk really believes he is an owl and insists we take him seriously. To make his point he can occasionally be seen crunching a live mouse between his molars. Poor man.

Bella reminds me more and more of a half-demented streetwalker I once met in Piraeus who collected her customers' sperm in buckets and bottles to sell by the gallon to a cosmetic laboratory in Marseille. Bella is constantly surrounded by a court of 'notables' who have bribed their way into her bedroom in anticipation of the 'special events' she promises. After entertaining all the male members of the ruling classes of G'NAAUU, not to mention their wives and daughters, with her special charm, she has now reached the point where she prefers midgets, lepers and cripples in bed. Her ideal man, she muses, is still to be born and would have to be as powerful as Ghengis Khan and as handsome as

Leslie Howard! She thinks men are hairy females with elongated sex organs or a bearded species of women. Left to herself she'd have all men's noses ringed. Whether she is certifiable, as Trevor claims, I can't say. She has recently certainly developed an eerie laugh. Quite uncanny. Bella's true love is Tara, the former mistress of a famous Enu general, who first lived with Burk but couldn't stand his habit of poking a finger up his own anus and constantly sniffing at it (so she said). At Bella's court Tara played dangerous sado-masochistic games for a while and only returned home to her estranged husband when she became very ill. She had contracted a weird infection on the inner part of her left thigh which would not heal. Enu surgeons (using claws and teeth for surgery, a practice condemned by their own medical association) were about to take her leg off. Tara went home and Bella was left alone for a while and brooded silently, addressing herself in the third person.

Trevor, to judge by his toothless grin, claims to be living in perfect marital bliss with his mistress, Guaka, another general's wife, who has forced him to remove all his teeth or stay away from her three-inch long nipples. The local methods of tooth extraction are pre-medieval. The dentist and his assistant make house calls when pulling teeth. The patient is tied to a chair and each of his teeth is knocked out separately with a small hammer. Why Trevor allowed this puzzled me at first, but when his gums had stopped bleeding he explained that he considered it a modest price to pay for perfect bliss. He calls her his 'Minerva', his 'Goddess of Wisdom', who has taught him that physical pain can be the ultimate redemption from insanity. When I tell him I think he is definitely mad he just smiles at me sympathetically.

Tibor is probably at a more advanced stage than the rest of us. Believing he could improve on local ingenuity, he began eating his own excrement. We had to remove him from the stove by force and lock him away for a few days without food. He recovered, but we wouldn't let him back into the kitchen, as we could never trust him again, not after what he did in front of our very eyes to a perfectly delicious Vichysoisse.

Sylvia was too absent-minded to understand what was going on, when we carried Tibor up to the attic. She babbles to herself most of the time or talks to her neighbours at 44 Rudfield Gardens, Highgate, complaining that she has trusted them all these years, but now realizes they have come to rob her flat and kill her cat Chocolate Mousse or 'Mouse'.

When I listen to my companions I am convinced I am in excellent mental and physical health. Admittedly this feeling has always been with me, even back in our normal, ordinary world in the company of my normal, ordinary friends.

Five

It has been my conviction all along that only an earthquake, a flood or a war could change our situation. I have proved to be right. It is thanks to the war between the Enu, the DUPA and the HURRU that I am here to tell my tale.

A few days after the PAKO has gone to put in his report we are having our normal afternoon tea on the western verandah, where at this time of the day the giant acacia spreads its shade, when my personal supervisor, Ango-Tak enters with a flushed and excited face and tells us a caravan of officials has arrived. She has led them to the reception rooms near the main gate where they are waiting for me to come down. As we are all more or less naked with only short pieces of cloth wrapped around us, Ango-Tak insists I should get dressed and not appear naked before the top brass who, though naked themselves, don't appreciate seeing us foreigners in the nude. She tells me to put on my best muslin shirt (the one her mother had made for me especially).

I do as she tells me and go downstairs immediately where I find an Enu named Pautok in the company of at least a dozen high-ranking officers and civil servants. Pautok, who is Defence Minister, is probably the most feared man in the country. He is known to have a penchant for war and also known to be the silent but not so secret enemy of the King, who for all his muscle, wants only to rule over a peaceful land, where he can peacefully pursue his favourite sport – the royal hunt. The King is said to hate war, because it closes entire provinces to his dogs and hunting companions, and for this he is branded a coward.

In Pautok's company is a fat and fairly jolly-looking man, called Maulok, the Foreign Minister, who has just returned from a diplomatic mission to QUIVOK, the capital of the HURRU. Maulok wears his fat buzzard with much dignity, gives me a big friendly grin and, while he might have a lot to say for himself, leaves the talking to his colleague. Pautok has a quiet, inwardly directed presence. He is suave, alert and correct. His eyes are cold and clever, the eyes of a mountain goat. He places his handsome red, yellow and black macaw next to Maulok's buzzard on a portable MULANA (a large basket specially made for this purpose), as is the custom inside a house or compound. All stare at me for a long while until Pautok finally breaks the silence. I had expected people would not bother with small talk down here. I was wrong. Pautok begins with generalities about his wife, sons and daughters, all highly educated, beautiful and successful (modesty is not a custom among the Enu and is considered bad taste). He finally comes to the point.

'Frankly, our situation is serious, whether or not this is obvious to you. It is a fact all the same. We are preparing for an important military operation and may need your help. War has been going on here for quite some time, as you must have learned by now. Our citizens are ignorant of this and believe in the peace they can see in the street. They love peace and do not expect war, and because they are unused to confronting war they have become lethargic and indolent. All this is going to change soon. War is a people's collective will to survive and should be out in the open, for all to see, for all to participate in. War is the stuff of life. Peace, its opposite, is a deflated useless time and ultimately we all suffer the mental agonies it entails, the greatest of which is boredom.'

All this sounds very familiar.

'What else is new, your Excellency? I have heard all this before. What you have just said is common knowledge.'

He continues, unperturbed by my interruption, to explain what he called 'the many virtues the bitterness of war produces' and compared them to 'the sweet-smelling but short-lived flowers of peace'. He fails to convince me.

I tell him I have heard all *this* before as well and that it is all the same to me if the Enu and HURRU and DUPA and GUKO and whatever they might call themselves decide to cut each other's throats, just the way they do where I come from. I have had six years of World War II and prefer to stay bored in my hammock rather than end up dead or maimed. Nor do I need to prove my courage, thank you very much.

'We hoped you foreigners might be of help, just because you might have seen action.'

Again I interrupt him and tell him my mind on this subject.

'After Hitler there seems to be no one worth fighting against. The Argentine colonels have nothing to fear from outside interference. Nor has a Pinochet in Chile – or an Ayatollah or Gaddafi – or a Brezhnev or Botha. And while our liberalism forbids us to interfere with the tyranny of other nations, we ourselves are not all that innocent either. We believe with the Reagans, the Schmidts, the Mitterands and the Thatchers that we ought to arm ourselves and then arm ourselves some more in order to show the Russians they have no chance. We even are willing to give arms to the Chinese, as long as they claim to hate the Russians. All this is total insanity. The Russians have neither the strength nor the ideology to conquer the world. They are backward in supplying the needs of twentieth and twenty-first century man – which is more and not less comfort and convenience, more automation and more electronic labour-saving devices that will ultimately fulfil our dream, which is to enjoy the pleasure and beauty our brief existence offers to all those who are chosen to see and taste for themselves how good it is. It is not the Russians we must fight but the stupidity of those idiots who overrate the Soviet power of evil and underrate their own. I believe that within a few years we might see in Russia a similar kind of change as happened silently in Spain and Portugal after forty years of repressive government. No revolution, no civil war, nothing of the kind. The same will take place in Russia and it is better to invest our money neither in butter nor in guns – both can kill you – but in eradicating the ignorance, poverty and repression which are still widespread and planting gardens in the Sahara and the Gobi deserts.'

'But what for?'

'Instead of sending our young men to war. Didn't you say you have a problem with all these idle youngsters?'

'The truth is – and you may find this hard to accept – we *want* to kill them off because we hate them for surviving us. It's the simple truth. What do you people do with your mobs of young and not-so-young men who are bored out of their minds? They don't care a fart for the future, have no memories, wish to make no sacrifices, want to give up nothing, neither property nor health, neither their own lives nor the lives of their families? All they do is gripe and complain and ask for softer mattresses to rest their fat arses on.'

I tell him we have exactly the same situation, but consider a third world war would be ill advised because its outcome is predictable and definitely disastrous. Hence, where I come from, we prefer cold war which is mainly talk, to the big nuclear heat.

'The fear of being afraid is worse than fear,' Pautok quotes one of his sages and continues: 'Besides there are no nuclear arms around here. All our fighting is done in the traditional style of pumas, using only teeth and nails.'

He disagrees with the PAKO's determinist legend of Enu ancestors deliberately blowing up their own nuclear arsenal and swears by what he calls an 'up-to-date' interpretation of history, which postulates a 'big bang' theory. Philosophically he can only admit of two alternatives, accident or determination, and continues: 'But one way or another, as you see, nothing is ever as bad as we imagine. Look at us! We have survived the atomic fireworks pretty well. As you may have noticed, there isn't that much difference between you and me, when you look at us. Amazing, ain't it?'

I look at him again – and again. Except for his nudity

and his painted-on decorations, his bare feet and the great number of charms he wears, he looks very much like all soldier-politicians anywhere in the world. He is cool, cynical and matter-of-fact in his approach to all questions concerning politics. He calls his king a liar, a traitor, a thief and a whore, and the mirror image of the man in the street who elected him. He goes on in this vein, describing in poetic language how life can ultimately only be enjoyed on the brink of disasters, which we first dream up, then think possible, and ultimately proceed to make come true. Why this should be so he cannot tell.

'Let's say that a Phoenix which rises from nuclear ashes will be no lovebird but will look more like one of the vultures we have circling overhead night and day.'

If the Enu want to make war we are in no position to stop them. As long as everything stays as 'normal' as it has been so far, we shall die here either of liver or of heart ailments, brought on by melancholy, leading to kidney failure. Meanwhile we are buried alive. The only way to get out is by stealth and deceit. Escaping is most likely doomed to failure. Certainly we can never get across the sea.

Our best bet is to try to desert to the enemy at the first opportunity. That much is clear. We'll have to take it from there, play it by ear.

I think it might help to fan his enthusiasm with a little theory: Von Clausewitz had called war *'an inherent necessity'*, *'a contradiction in itself* and *'an act of violence intended to compel our opponent to fulfil our will'*. ' *"War is nothing,"* ' I tell them, ' *"but a duel on an extended scale. If we would conceive as a unit the countless numbers of duels which make up a war, we shall do so best by supposing to ourselves two wrestlers. Each strives by physical force to compel the other to submit to his will: each endeavours to throw his adversary and thus render him incapable of further resistance. WAR IS THEREFORE AN ACT OF VIOLENCE INTENDED TO COMPEL OUR OPPONENT TO FULFIL OUR WILL. Violence arms itself with the inventions of Art and Science in order to contend against violence. Self-imposed restric-*

tions, almost imperceptible and hardly worth mentioning, termed usages of international law, accompany it without essentially impairing its power. Violence, that is to say, physical force (for there is no moral force without the conception of states and law), is therefore the MEANS. The compulsory submission of the enemy to our will is the ultimate object. In order to obtain this object fully, the enemy must be disarmed and disarmament becomes therefore the immediate object of hostilities in theory. It takes the place of the final object and puts it aside as something we can eliminate from our calculation." '

These few mouthfuls of Clausewitz, which have fed many generations of aspiring officers at the Frunze Academy, as well as at Sandhurst and West Point, go down with the Enu like sweet liqueur and Pautok begs me to quote them some more, so his younger adjutants can learn a thing or two. I have fortunately done my homework and continue to quote, just as if I were reading it to them from the printed page in J. J. Graham's translation from the original German.

' *"Now philanthropists may easily imagine there is a skilful method of disarming and overcoming an enemy without causing great bloodshed and that is the proper tendency of the art of war. However plausible this may appear, it is still an error which must be eliminated: for in such dangerous things as war, the errors which proceed from a spirit of benevolence are the worst. As the use of physical power to the utmost extent by no means excludes the co-operation of intelligence, it follows that he who uses force unsparingly, without reference to the bloodshed involved, must obtain a superiority if his adversary uses less vigour in its application. The former then dictates the rule to the latter and both proceed to extremities to which the only limitations are those imposed by the amount of counteracting force on each side."* '

As I expected, I am addressing the right audience and they beseech me to give them more of the same.

' *"If the wars of civilized people are less cruel and destructive than those of savages, the difference arises from the social condition of both states in themselves and in their relation to each other. Two motives lead men to war: instinctive hostility and hostile intention. It is impossible to conceive the passion of hatred of the wildest description, bordering on mere instinct, without combining it with the idea of hostile intention. On the other hand, hostile intentions may often exist without being accompanied by any, or at all events by extreme hostility of feelings. Among savages views emanating from the feelings, amongst civilized nations those emanating from the understanding, have the predominance, but this difference arises from the attendant circumstances, existing institutions etc. and therefore is not to be found necessarily in all cases, although it prevails in the majority. In short even the most civilized nations may burn with passionate hatred for each other."* '

To judge by their expression they are hypnotized by the wisdom of this Prussian Junker, who so obviously knew what war is all about and has a lot to teach most professional warriors.

'More, more,' they beg me in unison. Well, I, too, am getting caught up by the spirit of the moment and, had they begged me to stop, I couldn't have stopped.

' *"We may see from this,"* ' (I go on quoting), ' *"what a fallacy it would be to refer the war of a civilized nation entirely to an intelligent act on the part of the government, and to imagine it as continually freeing itself more and more from all feeling of passion in such a way that at last the physical masses of combatants would no longer be required; in reality their mere reaction would suffice – a kind of algebraic action . . . If war is an ACT of force it belongs necessarily also to the feelings. If it does not originate in the feelings, it REACTS more or less upon them and the extent of this reaction depends not on the degree of civilization but upon the importance and duration of the interests involved. Therefore we find civilized nations do not put their prisoners to death and do not devastate towns and countries, this is because their intelligence exercises greater influence on their mode of carrying on war, and has taught them more effectual means of applying force than these rude acts of mere instincts . . ."* ' '

'Are you saying you people make wars without putting your prisoners to death, without devastating the cities of your enemies? It doesn't quite follow from what you have quoted us before.'

'This was written in 1811 or so, a century before World Wars I and II. Don't worry. We have got back to our savage instincts, as the general called them, and this general was a wise philosopher to boot. Let me finish in his words, more informative than anything I have to say on the subject, as I am merely a traveller and writer and neither a philosopher nor a general. "*The constant progress of improvements in construction of weapons is sufficient proof that the tendency to destroy the adversary which lies at the bottom of the conception of war is in no way changed or modified through the progress of civilization.*" '

I feel they have had enough of that today. I have given them plenty to think about.

Pautok rises and so do the rest of the company and they line up to say 'goodbye' with increased respect before the application of so much unshakeable military logic to such a simple thing as a massacre.

'The kind of things we think about a lot and discuss in our military schools but never manage to express so eloquently.'

They all thank me once more for the 'most valuable insights' they have gathered today and leave.

Later in the evening I ask Ango-Tak what kind of enemies the Enu are about to fight. She mentions guerilla gangs called DUPA which are recruited from among their females and led by a legendary female general called Tunkapot. Yet she feels the legions of DUPA present no real danger to Enu authority, even though they cause a lot of nuisance and tension when interfering in personal feuds between husband and wife, father and daughter. Fist fights over the smallest incident are not uncommon between these women and the male defenders of law and order. The bulk of Tunkapot's army, she tells me, lives somewhere in the mountains. Male travellers found castrated in bed in one of the many Travellers' Inns which are all over the country, or murdered while performing their patriotic duty in the privy – all these random killings, credited to Tunkapot's ladies and their witchcraft, are 'as everyone knows' not the work of the women. Behind them is the sinister hand of the HURRU, an evil race of people if ever there was one. Ango-Tak knows very little about them.

'All they told us at school was: they live to the south-east and speak a language called ALGEBRA, consisting of incomprehensible numbers and letters no one can decipher. The HURRU are a mysterious race of sorcerers and necromancers and have contributed to our feelings of shame and inadequacy by creating in our minds the idea of a cardinal sin which supposedly besets everyone who is not one of their kind.

'An Enu who feels guilty for not being a HURRU must fight them, of course, as long as he believes in his own identity and the HURRU must outwit the Enu if they wish to survive. In every single war over the past forty years the numerically smaller HURRU tribe has beaten the overwhelming numbers of their adversaries and no one has ever figured out how. One of their superior tricks is to move the border while the fighting is still taking place. You believe you are driving them out before you, while in fact they have infiltrated your rear lines and are chasing you. Let's say we march into HURRU territory and they run away from us. We have done it many times: every time they disappear, the very same people you think have vanished have in fact moved after you to the same area, even into your street and are living right across the corridor. Only Providence, which occasionally sends us a strong leader, can put a stop to their slimy tricks. Our army seems for ever to be moving in circles. How do you explain that?'

What she has to say about the HURRU sounds not unfamiliar but still quite interesting, as one would never have expected that in this far corner of the world everything would be just like it is at home. Ango-Tak has only one solution to the problem of the powerful losing out against the weak and this solution is piety. Modesty. She would like to teach every Enu to speak in modest terms about himself, to follow the example of his enemy who behaves and speaks modestly to the Enu and only brags at home among his own kind about his feats of courage. The Enu on the other hand brags always. Both at home and towards others.

'They call themselves weak and defenceless and we should

do the same. The trick is to call yourself small and weak, don't you see?'

Her prejudices sound like all prejudices on the subject of minorities and I am no longer surprised when she tells me that HURRU (from 'to hurry', from being always on the move – the Enu liken them to squirrels) is but one of their many names; they are also known as NINNIES and SISSIES, SOFT EGGS and MEAN BASTARDS, PINKS and REDS, CRACKPOTS and COWARDS, ARSELICKERS and FAGGOTS, JEWS and NIGGERS, POUFFS and PAKIS, WOGS and FROGS and a few other familiar epithets. Her own people, according to her, are not much better but are indolent by nature, dress up like women (as soon as they can afford it!), use cosmetics and learn belly-dancing and knitting and ultimately turn faggot and impotent.

'Our men prefer masturbation to fornication. Can you understand that? I bet it's different where you come from.'

I have to disappoint her and relate Trevor's theory that the FBI and CIA spread hard and soft porn among the people, and that their secret new director, Hugh Hefner, shares with Herbert Hoover more than just his initials – namely a religious concern to bring the western birthrate down. To quote Trevor: '*Playboy* magazine gives us an all-revealing look into the womb whence all our trouble stems from.'

Let me report to her credit that she does not really believe Trevor's theory of the big porno plot cooked up by Opus Dei, the MOSSAD, the CIA and the KGB, with Hefner's FBI left to carry it out. She thinks Trevor's claim that Hugh Hefner and his confederates at *Penthouse* and *Hustler*, who appeal to the boy in the man and ask a man to play instead of seriously adding to an excessive overpopulation, is a lot of nonsense. I am not so sure she is right here, but why argue everything?

Ango-Tak is the perfect partner to talk to and there is no doubt in my mind or hers that if I were to leave she would come with me wherever I go. Should we get caught our future would look grim and this additional danger adds even more excitement to our amorous bond.

Let me admit it: after many months among the exotic Enu, I have discovered that inside their minds they are as exotic as my neighbours at home. After this disillusionment the company of this strange and savage girl is titillating. She loves love with a devotion none of my friends have for the subject matter we might be discussing.

Now that we live in grand style many famous and illustrious brains drop by on the slightest pretext in order to waste their time and ours with philosophical speculation and opinionated garbage, probably to escape their families for a little while. By the end of every such intellectual encounter I am more convinced than ever I really want to get away from here and the sooner the better.

Six

A mere twenty feet below my terrace the wilderness begins and stretches until the far away horizon. Across a gorge to my right descends a waterfall, a sheet of water, polished and transparent like plate glass, clearly revealing the rock formations behind. The water drops a hundred feet to a point where it turns into a turbulent foaming river. From where we are, we cannot see the river, but we can hear it loud and clear. Out here we are completely cut off from the other wings of the house where the windows are constantly open to the square, which is packed with noisy traders and even noisier orators; clever acrobats and solemn snake-charmers; jugglers and rope-dancers; fire-eaters and water-diviners; and other artists, entertaining a melancholy yawning crowd.

Up here, alone with Ango-Tak, I can hardly believe there are such characters as Trevor and Tibor, Burk, Sylvia and Bella, not to mention the hordes of argumentative natives worrying one another with all sorts of horror stories, usually ending in the popular assumption that the world is about to come to an end not with a bang but a big loud yawn. Up here all this seems remote and irrelevant.

A few lonely hawks, eagles and swallows circle the blue above the treetops, gliding by majestically in total silence, far from the noise and comforts of the town's aviary. These few wild predators spot, hunt and catch their prey in the old timeworn tradition. Watching them sail by makes me feel freedom is within reach.

Our escape plan involves rope-ladders and provisions and waiting patiently for the new moon when the nights will be so pitch dark that no right-minded Enu (who would dread to leave the walls of his city even at full moon), would set a foot outside the gates to go after us. We plan to cross a ford over the EVRA together with the buffaloes and from territory presently occupied by the rebel women we shall make our way to the wind tunnel which is the official border between the Enu and HURRU LAND. With a bit of luck and clever arguments we shall persuade the HURRU to build us a ship or raft, which we shall sail up the coast to collect the rest of my friends. We don't mention our plans to anyone. The risk of being betrayed is too great.

Meanwhile we are in love, just like Amor and Psyche. I gradually begin to unravel this strange woman's mind. It opens up to my passionate interest in her with an abundance of revealing little details. Whether it is the silence or the meticulous attention she pays to what I say, my mind sails back to London, to a shelf in front of my bathroom mirror and a small bottle of tiny yellow tablets my doctor, Tony Greenburgh, gave me to be taken against sea-sickness. At moments I believe I must have swallowed all thirty-two Dramamins at one gulp and washed them down with a few small shots of cognac. On the other hand if the bottle remained untouched (and I can't be certain of that) my mind is capable of producing this present hallucinogenic state all by itself. In that case my attempt to escape must end as disastrously as my innocent visit to Crownflights in Baker Street, when I could not have foreseen what subsequently became horrendous reality.

On attempting to leave the country in the company of an alien without an exit permit the local laws are similar to those in Saudi Arabia. Ango-Tak will be stoned to death and I shall see my head rolling away from the rest of my body and inside this head I shall be wondering whether this adventure had been worth while after all. 'To leave the known for the unknown is a big temptation – for fools like myself,' will probably be my final thought.

*

The same night I have a curious dream in which Pautok sticks his head round my door and calls out loud: 'Coronation'. Moments later I am carried by four strong men who dump me into a bathtub, where I get the attention of half a dozen young and attractive women who go to work on me with brushes, soap and endless buckets of hot water. Then I'm being dried, oiled, powdered and bundled into silk. A small army of barbers and their assistants curl my hair with hot irons, put make-up on my face, many different rings on each finger and claws over my nails. In the mirror I look like the spit and image of the King, as I remember him on his turtle, except that I am half his size and half his weight, a younger version of the same. A silvery stovepipe is placed over my head with a visor cut out in front. The pipe is heavy, smells of bird droppings and pulls my eyes down.

A voice says: 'We thought of putting an ostrich on top of you but decided you would soon turn into one.'

'Who is we?' I hear myself asking.

'We is we. We is the Enu. We is the people. We decided on a macaw instead.'

'If you say so.'

'The bird will find it a little hard to settle down at first, because you might still be a bit shaky on your legs. These birds, remember, are very sensitive. If you feel weak at the knees, the birds feel nervous. If your stomach gets upset – God help you. Switch off your mind. One stupid idea and it might even die on you.'

'Die from one stupid thought?'

'That's how sensitive they are. It would be a very bad omen. The people might lynch you on the spot. Don't think. Stupid thoughts may cost you your life.'

He kisses me across the shoulder, first one side, then the other. I walk over bare backs, smiling benignly like a somnambulist.

'Sit down and be quiet!'

I can do nothing else. I sit down on an elaborate carved throne made either of human bones or of ivory. I can't say.

How did I ever get here? What happened? Why did these bastards have to pick on me? I straighten my spine. All thought vanishes. I hear the gurgling prayers and incantations spoken in OUNGOUL. A creek rushing through a canyon. A huge macaw, striped red and yellow, with a beak as large as its body, is placed on top of the contraption on my head. It rustles its feathers and tries to find its place. I feel it down to my fingertips. When the bird is moving no longer, I feel it down to my toes. I stretch them, press them lightly all the way down and finally feel at ease. My feet touch solid ribbons of spines and necks. More chanting and more prayers. Voices are raised. Hands are lifted to the sky.

Hundreds and thousands of birds released from cages hover and flutter up into the blue and circle above us. The priest says a final; 'Amen' and the crowds shout 'HOWYU'. The singing of patriotic hymns. Priest and assistant take their place behind the throne. A trumpet thunders. A bugle calls. Drums rattle. Arms are presented, showing their dirty finger nails. Once more the crowd yells 'Long live the King!' They all stare in my direction and I can say nothing, I cannot even smile with this load on my head. I cannot and must not move. The parade passes before the throne. Uniformed cripples. Uniformed hunchbacks. Uniformed lepers and mental patients in uniform. The spastics and epileptics, the amputated and the blind, they all wear their own uniforms and have their own insignia and flags and mascots.

'We allow this once a year,' the priest bends over to me. 'Then all of them vanish and we won't have to see them again. But once a year we think it's good for them, and maybe good for us too.'

The parade is followed by a grand reception where the élite of the country meet in fancy dress. Glass instruments play silvery tunes. The tangerines taste of cherries and everyone compliments me on my feathered friend in my 'loft' and says nice things about it. What a handsome bird, people say. A kaleidoscope of colours.

The circus begins. Prolonged applause. The music blares.

Three elephants come galloping into the arena. A few minutes later a whistle blows and three horses storm in; the horses jump on the backs of the elephants and round and round they go. A gay and happy melodious tune. Again a whistle, three dogs come charging in, run straight up the backs of the elephants and the horses and have hardly sat down when the music gets louder and four cats fly in and climb on top of the dogs, and round and round they go. After a few rounds, three grey mice run up the galloping elephants' legs, up the horses, up the dogs, up the cats' tails on their hindlegs. One more whistle, three tiny birds flutter on to the heads of the grey mice and perch up there, and, as if that weren't enough, three butterflies make for the backs of the tiny birds and round and round they go. The audience is delirious and it's surely enough, this is real circus. But no: after the clapping and the stamping dies down, a small voice whispers loudly: 'Other way round,' and the unbelievable happens: round the arena flutter three elephants on the backs of the butterflies, just like a merry-go-round. The audience roars. The music blares. It's called PATAPARUKA.

What a show! What a dream!

I wake up. It's late in the morning – my breakfast is cold by now.

Two days later, I am still wondering whether or not such a vivid dream must forecast an imminent high drama (for which I feel ill prepared) when Pautok reappears. This time he comes unexpected and unannounced and accompanied by two bodyguards only. He introduces them as his *aides-de-camp*. After my impressive and lengthy quotations from Clausewitz, Pautok is convinced he has found in me his military expert and I admit I am flattered. First time a sensible man has come to ask my advice on how to conduct a successful military campaign – which offers me a chance to give him a host of views I hold on this and various other subjects and the perfect topic to camouflage our plan. By now I am convinced that whatever I needed to learn from this brief insight into the mentality of the natives on this remote island I have now learned. A society no longer pre-occupied with the elementary prose of existence, like eating, drinking and excreting, will still be ready to wage stupid wars. It is all too familiar. The same everywhere. Six months of it is quite enough. It's time to go home. I should never have left it.

Go? Yes, but how? My friends don't see it my way. They think to return to England makes no sense. We have discovered, they suggest, a way of life here, no Western standard of living offers us.

'I might be bored,' Trevor argues, 'but I am no more bored here than I am back in London. If it's the same everywhere, anyway, why leave? Nothing is exciting. Speaking for myself I have seen it all. It's the same shit everywhere, but here at least it tastes good. That's why I'm staying.'

Burk, far away in his owl-like posture, from which he hardly moves, except for an occasional attempt to fly down the stairs, which usually ends in loud screams, also refuses to go. The very idea makes him laugh, he hoots.

Tibor believes he has found his paradise: people, food, time, women and more women than he needs. No taxes. No cars. No effort. 'Sleeping, eating, existing is plenty of work. I don't know what you want to do in London, but you may leave me here.'

Sylvia, of course, cannot be separated from her husband. Bella, as I mentioned before, is too entrenched in her bed ever to leave it. When not making love, she now spends her time being massaged and combed. She loves to lounge and can think of no lazier life than here among the Enu. Her mind is made up. She tells me I should not even try to persuade her. 'What is better than being lazy?'

Pautok explains his strategy and wants my comment. 'If I say we are going to attack the HURRU, the DUPA will think we'll attack them instead, that's why we shall operate against them simultaneously, but not involve ourselves too seriously.

More noise than battle. Meanwhile we'll march on QUIVOK. What would your Prussian general say to this?'

I remind him that Von Clausewitz made it quite clear that war is conducted to 'compel our adversary to fulfil our will' but if there is no will to be fulfilled war makes no sense. It might make sense for me and for Ango-Tak, who want to get away but this I don't tell him.

'How about you coming along on this operation to watch what we do? You might learn how we do it here. Tomorrow night after sunset the first infantry brigade moves towards the EVRA and blocks all their supply routes. Siege to be completed before sunrise. We intend to stay a week. After a week they'll have to break out to get fresh provisions. We'll capture a few, maybe only a dozen. Meanwhile my second army brigade will move south and assault the famous wind tunnel, which we'll take from them this time, so help me God, even at great cost. I don't intend to launch a protracted war. In four weeks the campaign will be over and we'll have achieved all our objectives. We shall have humiliated the DUPA, making them less reliable partners for our enemy, and by conquering the tunnel, and making a limited and restrained incursion into their territory (which was ours originally!) we shall have proven our superiority. And that's all we need to prove. This lesson will not be lost on them when we later start colonizing our liberated territory, with our own people.'

'First things first. How do you fight women?'

'First we hypnotize them. Then we net them. Then we bite. We put our teeth in them until they scream. We wrestle them to the ground. No rape. We bundle them up, take them home, where they belong, treat them well and keep an eye on them. After six months or so, once they are used to being back again, we let them out. Meanwhile we'll have brainwashed them and showered them with presents, until they are content. We buy them slaves.'

'Buy them slaves?'

'Of course. Men love working but no woman ever does. Not if they can help it. Women love to have maids, preferably female slaves, at their beck and call. They prefer them beautiful, of course, but better an unattractive slave than none. Our economic system, as you may know, is based on the distribution of wealth at birth. All male children receive a state pension at birth. Not our females – only we males. If we granted females the same, which is what they want, they would share authority with us which is bad for our male ego. Our male ego is the ultimate energy which turns the world and nothing else. Our ego drives the universe. Without our ego we are lost. Nothing must be done to undermine it. It should be strengthened and never weakened; men are weak enough as it is. After five lost wars, we have lost confidence in ourselves. Surprised?'

'Why fight wars you lose?'

'Because to win a war is not always a blessing. To win a battle here and there is quite enough. Win a war and you have to make the enemy do your will, as your master Clausewitz says. What will? We have no will. We even lack a will to live. We no longer need it. We are part of a big machine. We are the machine. What we need is excitement. That's all. The rest takes care of itself.'

All things take their course in time. We have been waiting for a chance to get closer to the border and here it is. If Pautok wants me to come along, he will have to let me take Ango-Tak with me. His master plan to confuse his enemies will flop, of course, and his army will be beaten once more. All the same, I'm ready and impatient to move. Pautok, before leaving, mentions casually that we might soon expect the King to abdicate in favour of a regent who will, in time, make way for a new monarch – one who enjoys the confidence of all his people. When I hear this kind of familiar intrigue by an ambitious politician I think it's time to pack up. A string of unbelievable events ensues before we leave.

The next morning we see from the windows regiments of young men marching off to battle with heroic tunes, rumbling drums and wailing trumpets, followed by large flocks of birds and relatives. For a long time an eerie silence hangs over the town. For once the square seems to be empty except for a few nervous guards who pace up and down before the gates of the palace. Then, as if by command, people stream into the square from all directions, shout slogans, scream murder and yell revenge. The mob grows rapidly like a swarm of locusts. Again as if by command, young and old men attack the gates and are beaten back. Water canons and tear gas are used on the crowd of extras which swells as if some unseen director were prompting more of them to get out on stage.

What is happening is shouted from roof to roof: though Pautok had urged the King to declare war, the King refused. He and his family and close servants were then immediately put under arrest. Then Pautok sent his men to the HURRU Embassy and took all one hundred and twenty of them, both staff and diplomatic corps, away in chains and brought them to the military prison he keeps in the basement of his own residence. Once the news of the arrest of the enemy aliens had spread, two things happened more or less simultaneously: the HURRU began invading Enu territory with the object of liberating their countrymen and the local police were alerted to intervene firmly against a frenzied mass of citizens who were converging on the palace, urged on by Pautok's very own *agents provocateurs*. The situation seemed to be getting out of hand. Within the first few hours, there was a risk that law and order would break down and a danger that unforeseen developments might force Pautok to hand the King and his family over to the mob for a public lynching, which could have led to all kinds of even more difficult demands by the deeply confused and disturbed masses.

From a sleepy and yawning backwater all of a sudden G'NAAUU has turned into a turbulent sea. Faces have lost their dullness, everyone seems to be lit up with some incomprehensible fanaticism in his eyes. Around lunch time there is a little lull in the feverish activities that are going on all over town and, as I am about to close the window to go back to my peaceful terrace, four men grab me, blindfold me and whisk me away. I feel something like a pinprick in my right arm, seconds later my face and all my limbs begin to glow and burn as if I had been set alight. I hear Ango-Tak calling for me, her voice comes from very far away. Burning wings carry me into a windowless enclosure filled with ice and snow. Pautok enters through a locked door without turning a key. He is dressed like the priest in my dream, takes my hand and commands: 'Coronation'. What follows is an unbelievable repetition of my dream of a few nights ago. After the coronation I am asked to step outside on the balcony (I seem to be in the palace) and can see the façade of our prison across the square and below me a mass of thousands of screaming and dancing savages who keep on yelling 'ITITITITIT!' which, I take it, is the name of their King.

A quick glance in through the French windows of the balcony convinces me that I look like their King. Pautok, who stands next to me, shouts something in OUNGOUL and GOULGOUL to say that on the people's behalf he has accepted the King's offer to return all power back to them. Now that war has been declared the first reports from the front tell of heavy casualties among the savage enemy who will soon be forced to sue for peace. There is a long and all-enveloping roar of 'Hurray' rising from below. All I have to do is wave and grin.

Pautok doesn't leave it at that. He tells the people that a new law has come into effect: for the first time all the members of the families of everyone who is called up will also be enlisted. The new army is going to be truly a people's army and the logistics for its supply are not more complicated than those of feeding a civilian population at home. Why indeed should only the young men be forced to lay down their lives for their beloved country? The dying soldier at the front will draw comfort from seeing familiar faces around him. The masses agree completely.

On the back of the royal turtle they have erected an enclosure fit for a King and his consort. Next to me lies Ango-Tak (I refused to leave her behind and Pautok had no choice but to give in). To pass the time I tell her how differently we people in Europe and the rest of the world go to war, with terrible flying machines, which swoop down at the speed of sound and throw bombs the size of mansions. A few dozen of them can easily devastate an entire town within half an hour – and this by using old-fashioned explosives. She looks blank. To amuse her I tell her that we too, ordinary civilians, can fly with such huge birds which we call 'aeroplanes'. We enter these birds through their ribcages or their anus by means of a ladder taller than the acacia in our yard. These birds carry passengers and their luggage across continents. Their flesh, bones and feathers are made of aluminium, plastic materials, steel and glass. As soon as we are on board we are made to sit down in comfortable armchairs and must neither smoke cigarettes nor strike matches before take-off. While standing on the ground the bird is fed with a highly explosive liquid via a fat tapeworm. A few drops of such liquid would kill an ordinary bird but these large fowl can't get enough of it and drink it by the ton. They stand on round legs called 'wheels'. Once all passengers are seated and the doors back and front are locked, the bird exhales heavy black fumes and rolls slowly towards a wide field. Its roar becomes louder, wheels roll faster. It runs for miles on these rounded legs and suddenly lifts itself into the air. An animal, half the size of G'NAAUU's main street, rises into the clouds. In case it loses a wing, or its brain pops out, which happens from time to time, we are not allowed to untie ourselves from our seats during take-off and landing. Should the bird explode in mid-air we come sailing down in comfortable armchairs. Alas, because of earth's gravity the impact on the ground destroys both passengers and chair. Fortunately this happens rarely. Most of the time our birds fly above the clouds and over the highest mountain peaks, faster than it takes the earth to turn on its axis, with the unbelievable result of arriving at a place thousands of miles away hours before the time of departure.

Thirty-five thousand feet up in the air, we can walk, eat, drink and play cards. Mothers feed their babies and people can sleep as if they were at home in their beds. We can even use toilets. Wastes are collected in plastic bags and dropped when full, at great heights. Usually they land in the wilderness, but occasionally these frozen parcels crash through the roofs of poor people's homes and even the poorest among us do not appreciate such mysterious presents, though they would feed an entire household here in this country. The fact that these frozen stink bombs fall more frequently in the United States than elsewhere has caused serious speculation in Pentagon circles as to whether these so-called accidents are not in fact part of a wider plot by Russian and Lybian agents in Pan Am uniform, designed to fan a smell of malcontent in the suburbs of America's big cities. Investigation has so far not disproven this theory. Apart from this, flying in one of these birds is one of the great experiences of our civilization. The invention of flying for people has shrunk our globe to the size of one large city.

'If flying is so marvellous why didn't you come here with one of these superfowl?'

'Good question. The answer is: fate or destiny. Had the same troubles overcome us on a plane, ending with the vessel's explosion, none of us would ever have come out of it alive. The airlines supply chairs but no parachutes. I managed to swim ashore though I actually don't know how to swim.'

It was indeed a major miracle to have survived the recent disaster and I am fairly confident that the worst is behind me and that we might soon be sailing back to the normal world. Words make no sense here. To swim the sea is as unthinkable to her as to walk on the moon's surface would have been for our grandparents. In her heart neither she nor anyone else here believes we had in fact swum ashore. Even though hundreds of them must have watched us on the beach on that strange cool Sunday morning God knows how long ago.

Her suspicion that we had not swum ashore but been dispatched by submarine at the end of a rope or line, she found confirmed by this strange knot in the middle of my stomach. She had never seen a belly button in her life. When she queried me about it, I think the second or third time we were idling around in bed, I told her something about the navel string by which every human is attached to its mother's body. But she never believed this story either. The Enu have no navel because Enu are born inside the shell of an egg and emerge from their shells immediately after they leave their mother's womb. It's a moot philosophical point whether the Enu are viviparous, just like all mammals, or oviparous, like reptiles and birds. Maybe a combination of both is true. An Enu baby which does not open its eggshell from within is usually gobbled up by its parents and the other members of the family. A timeworn tradition, for which Ango-Tak, belonging to the revolutionary youth of her generation, no longer cares. Their debates about whether or not to eat their stillborn eggs are similar to our never-ending discussions on abortion, a permanent source of controversy. There are those who are for and those who are against it. Once in a million times it happens that an egg is opened with outside help, but this is rare. A deep-rooted taboo against touching these eggs leaves it to the newborn to 'decide' for himself whether or not he wishes to enter this world.

This stoic attitude towards their newborn has its parallel in the Enu way of looking at death. To say an Enu does not believe in death is to utter the absolute and exact truth. To start with, an Enu never sees anyone's death, because of an ancient tradition which makes death 'invisible'. The very old enter grottoes, subterranean old people's homes, and they might go on living down below for hundreds of years or until they run out of the medicine which they call BOTO. The same is true for the chronically ill. They wander off into clinics in remote parts of the country. Fatal diseases are uncommon. The new POK supposedly inoculates the consumer against all known infectious disease. All bacterial or viral inflammations are fought with a spoonful of POK. There are of course broken limbs and skulls, caused by accidents and war wounds. Yet death itself is rarely visible, meaning it is beyond most citizens' experience. It has no reality. You are either visible or not.

In a tradition also known to the Parsees of Bombay, the deceased are offered up to the vultures to help the dead man's shortcut to reintegration with nature, which in time reincarnates all living things. Death, therefore, seems as unimportant here as a visit to the dentist is with us, painful, perhaps, and sooner or later inevitable but hardly worth mentioning.

Thanatos has no sting and Eros offers little reason for excitement. To call the Enu licentious is an understatement. In theory, as well as in practice, an Enu performs the act of coitus any time and with anyone he wishes, by daylight, in public and even in the middle of traffic if he cares to and no one except children and perverts would bother to pay attention to it.

On our soft mattresses stuffed with hay, jogging along on the back of the ancient royal turtle we move at approximately one mile an hour and this is still too fast.

The five or ten miles to the river EVRA, our first stop, seems five hundred miles away, and we are not getting closer to our destination. It has taken me a little while to notice our uncanny horizon, situated slightly above eye level, a concave experience, as if one were lying at the bottom of a frying pan looking up towards its rim. From this particular perspective geometry makes really no sense and perhaps this explains why an Enu cannot grasp the meaning of distances.* They use numbers instead of adjectives. When an Enu says 'five people' he might mean something that has little to do with the word 'five'. He might mean lazy people or slow people or old people but not necessarily that there are five of them. Ango-Tak says we have maybe two miles to go. She means to

* And hence never develops numerals beyond the measure of his immediate vicinity.

say: It's only a short way from here but seems long to us –
because we are impatient to get there.

The day is hot, very hot; I fall asleep several times. Whenever I wake up I have a strange feeling, and I don't know
whether it is the heat or because we are in fact descending,
while apparently climbing, but the faces around me are
changing back into the more familiar appearance of bloated
reptiles on two human legs. Ango-Tak, too, shows unexpectedly the fangs of a sabre-toothed tiger. At moments
this attractive, sweet girl looks totally alien and savage to
me, something I have not seen in her all these past months.
Her forehead is smaller now, her ears more pointed, her
nostrils quiver, her voice changes into a growl. I convince
myself this is part of my hallucination I am about to escape.
Stranger still, she tells me stories in her new growling voice
about the female General Tunkapot, which make me feel
she is in love with her, more than that, besotted by her and
not in a lesbian erotic way, but more like a schoolgirl's
crush on her tennis idol. She gives her wonderful names like
'Queen of the Night', 'Princess' and 'Perfect Beauty' with
silken skin, violet eyes, long blonde hair, large white breasts,
brilliant ivory teeth, the curves of a goddess and the brains
of a sage' – but while she praises her, under her breath she
calls her also the most obscene and vulgar names, as if she
were talking about a precious best friend, a sister with whom
she quarrels.

In fact, she has never met her in the flesh, but is remember-
ing all the gossip and intrigues connected with her name.
Tunkapot must be twenty years older than herself because
Ango-Tak's mother when a young girl, remembers Tunkapot to have been a legend among women for her rejection of
the most powerful men in the country the moment they
wanted to marry her. While Ango-Tak tells me one unlikely
story after another, in which Tunkapot rapes men against
their will, destroys small children, rips female competitors to
pieces with her long claws and castrates her own father and
brother, and this kind of banter, I look out for signs of war

but can see none. The land seems asleep in a pastoral, tropical siesta. There is no evidence of pillage or arson, not a ruin or burned-down barn in sight. The spell of the female legions must have been powerful enough by itself to drive the Enu out of their wits. Invisibly operating amazons seems to be the right sort of phobia for local savages, and these begin to look more and more savage by the moment.

When we finally reach the EVRA late in the afternoon, shortly before sunset and I look down into the ravine, which carries large boulders in its turbulent foam with the roar of a deluge, and see the barren granite walls steeply ascending from both river banks, I understand: no one has ever crossed this gorge and whoever brags that he can will naturally be credited with sorcery and witchcraft.

We make camp for the night. Soon the entire plateau is alight with small fires in preparation for the evening meal. For a while the silver metallic voices of small children mix with the sound of kettles, the crackling of wood, the monotonous melodies of men and women around the roaring fires. Their faces are serious, even grim. Their eyes reduced to small slits. Their curled claws turn the spits and occasionally tear pieces of flesh off the slowly roasting goats and pigs. I am in the company of eerie creatures who look nothing like the by now familiar Enu.

Beyond the ravine, on the other side of the bank, a large orange moon moves over the volcano and drenches the night with its lugubrious flaming crystal ball.

A dark forbidding jungle rises up the slopes. Bats cruise overhead. The birds have gone to sleep and the fires gone out, one by one. The stars stand high and tiny, like tinsel spread over a black sheet of paper. Cries of monkeys and parrots. The howling of hyenas and jungle wolves and the hungry roar of black panthers in concert with bullfrogs, crickets and lovelorn nightingales. The flaps of my tent are open. Ango-Tak seems asleep, curled up like a large feline. Her head is tucked under her shoulder. I cannot imagine ever lying down with her again. I cannot sleep and look out and across to the mysterious volcano, listen to the noises of the night and wonder how we will ever make it across this ravine. Pautok suddenly stands next to me. From what I can see of him in the light of an orange moon he no longer has his introspective, intelligent face. He reminds me of a wild savage animal now, a puma, with yellow fluorescent burning eyes and whispers: 'Remember, we don't see them but they can see us. They have been waiting for us, know all our moves. When everyone has dozed off, shortly before dawn, they will attack. You won't hear them. They move on cats' paws. Should you hear anything, shout it out loud, don't be afraid, just scream. We all are wide awake and will be at your side immediately to help you. Call before it's too late.'

He steps back into the dark and has vanished, as if behind a screen.

I turn back into the tent. Ango-Tak must have been watching the two of us as we stood before the entrance. She is wide awake. I, too, seem to have woken up, alarmed by all that might still be ahead of us this night. Her body has changed rapidly, her hands and one of her feet have turned into paws. Her right foot still shows toes, but they change even while I look at them. Her arms and chest are covered with soft fur and so is part of her face. Her ears are pointed now, her eyes slanted and two large yellow marbles stare at me without blinking. She yawns and reveals the teeth of a young tiger and a long feline tongue, pink and red in the torchlight as if she had just dipped it in blood.

I am probably only imagining all this. She talks: 'Sit down. I'll tell you a story that might keep you awake. Remember not to close an eye tonight. It's time you woke up. I am telling you the story of Enunu, the ancestor of all the Enu. When Enunu still walked the earth he owned every stone, every tree, every animal and every living soul. His children were the stars and the favourites among them the sun and moon, but his best friend he called Night. And while he was debating the fate of the universe with his friend, Night (they shared a tent together just like we do), a hand appeared from outside and moved along the ground quickly just like a snake. Can you see it, can you?'

'Get to the end of your story,' I hear myself say. 'I can see no hand.'

I am lying because I do see a hand and it moves rapidly towards her, it slides along the ground, along her leg, up her torso towards her throat. As if the hand had been unscrewing a light bulb, it suddenly turns pitch dark. The torch has gone out. A storm blows, sending everything flying. Tent poles break like brittle bones, hides tear, ripped away like strips of paper. The tent falls on top of me. I have to use both arms and legs to free myself. I hear strange voices, laughing and giggling. Then the sound of crunching teeth and a long drawn out scream. I know it is Ango-Tak.

I want to call for help and can barely breathe. The night is as calm as before. Flickering torches in other tents, some only a few yards away, but no one seems disturbed. The sounds of quiet conversation, of laughter and singing. A few dogs bark far away and below, down in the ravine, the river rushes at its usual speed. Nothing has changed out here and when I turn round to see the wreck of the tent, the tent is standing there just as it was when we put it up the same afternoon but now it is filled with a white light. I look in to see what has happened. Ango-Tak has vanished. Where I saw her lying only a few minutes or so ago, now stands the legend which obviously destroyed her. She is as Ango-Tak has described her, fairly tall, has a lavish flow of golden hair, very beautiful eyes, the colour of azure. She looks at me, her lips are curled into a mysterious smile.

'Let's go now,' she says. Her voice is pleasant and calm.

'Go where?'

'Away from here.'

'But I am not here. I am on my balcony. I fell asleep, because of the heat. I am dreaming. I am asleep. The heat. Don't you feel the heat?'

Her face is closer now. I look into her eyes which are only inches removed from mine. They stand over me like two sentries and I know I shall remain their permanent prisoner. 'Let's go,' she says. 'You certainly can't stay here. Your time here is definitely over.'

Considering the alternatives, I had no choice and followed her.

After we had spent a few leisurely weeks in a small hut on the seashore with Tunkapot, a cargo boat, the SS *Paramaribo*, registered in Rotterdam, saw our smoke signals, picked us up and was ready to sail straight back to Auckland with its cargo of snakes, lizards, monkeys and rare birds destined for the zoos of Singapore and Penang. I insisted we should sail up the north coast because I had some friends there in prison. At the spot where we had originally come ashore, near the bay the Sorels had invaded, we dropped anchor and rode straight up and on to the beach in two motor launches equipped with radio transmitters. Our party was made up of twenty-four heavily armed officers and ratings. I expected to find everyone within a few hours either dead or alive. I led the party across the lagoon and along the path we were taken as prisoners by Colonel Black Eagle and his men. As we left shortly after dawn, we should have reached G'NAAUU by noon at the latest.

The island seemed totally deserted except for families of monkeys and baboons chasing each other through the branches overhead. There were no Enu and there was no G'NAAUU. They had vanished from the face of the earth and so, of course, had Trevor and Tibor, Bella, Burk and Sylvia. We spent all day wandering about and broke off the search when it turned dark and returned to the ship, exhausted but also disturbed. Except for Tunkapot, who looks just like many other very good-looking women, I had no means of proving whether or not there had been friends of mine kept in prison on this island or whether I had made it all up. The captain, officers and crew gave me strange looks and the ship's doctor, one Johan van der Agsterribbe, put me under heavy sedation until we reached Auckland three or four weeks later. We arrived in Auckland in the early hours of 11th December 1981 and I was back in London, at Heathrow Airport seventy-two hours later after an absence of one year, ten months and eleven days.

Back in London my first visit, of course, was to Crownflights in Baker Street. To my surprise the same clerk, John Farquharson, was standing in front of the very same poster where I had seen him last time. It read: 'Southampton–Sarawak–Southampton. £650 – no extras. COSMIC TAKES GOOD CARE OF YOU.'

John Farquharson looked a bit odd. His expression had changed. His eyes were reduced to two narrow slits and he looked at me out of these wild and savage eyes.

'I have now been waiting three hours for you to go home. I told you you can make up your mind by tomorrow. You don't have to pay now. But will you please leave?'

'I am here to complain,' I said firmly. 'This bloody *Katherine Medici* you advertise went down, don't you see, and so did everyone else – except for Trevor Lunt, Tibor and Sylvia Kovasc, Bella Karpakos and Burk Humpelman and when I looked for them they had vanished. What do you say to that?'

But he wouldn't listen and pushed me out with a loud grunt. Outside the rain had not stopped. If anything, it was raining even harder. I was definitely back in London. It took me a while to hail a taxi. As soon as I was back in my apartment I went straight to the typewriter to tell what had happened, whether or not I can be believed.